# The Roanoke Effect

# Chapter 1

My name is Blake Dornan, and it's been two years since the disappearances. I still have no idea what's going on, how it happened, or why. All I know is that everything and everyone I ever knew is gone. And I've just about reached my breaking point. I have never felt this alone, except for one time, when my...I still have a hard time mentioning it, even on paper.

Let me go back before the beginning, before the Nightmare started.

We lived in a decent sized town. A small city, really. Forty thousand people, give or take. It was a little bigger than what I liked, personally, but my wife was happy here. I had made a decent income as a writer. I didn't have any *New York Times* bestsellers, but I still made a good living. *Kirkus Reviews* had some nice things to say about my work, and my agent and publisher always seemed happy when I

Copyright©2024 David Nelson

All rights reserved. No part of this publication may be stored or introduced into a retrieval system, or transmitted in any form, or by any means, including, but not limited to, electronic, mechanical, photocopying, or recording, except for brief quotes used in a published review, without prior written permission from both the copyright owner and the publisher.

ISBN: 9798326515001

This is a work of fiction. Names, places, incidents, brands, media, and activities are a product of the author's imagination, or are used fictitiously. Any resemblance to actual persons, living or dead, is purely coincidental. The author acknowledges the trademark status and trademark owners of various products mentioned in this work of fiction, which have been used without permission. The publication or use of these trademarks is not authorized, associated with, or sponsored by the trademark owners.

moved upstairs. The doctors had had to put her under in order to get the pump tube down her throat. After they finished, they put meds in her IV, in addition to antibiotics, to keep her under for some time even after the tube had been removed. They said that was so her body could rest, due to the severity of the food poisoning. The nurse handed me Emily's clothes bag and gave me the floor and room number. I thanked her for everything she had done, and headed for the elevator.

"Ten-four," Mark said into the radio. Then to me, "They're ready for you now."

I ran inside. The lady security hit the door button when she saw me come in. She told me on the way which section and room to go to. An ER nurse was waiting for me.

"So what's going on?" I asked.

"It was severe food poisoning," the nurse replied, "so they went in to pump her stomach."

I felt my anger coming back. "And it took this long to figure that out?"

"Mr. Dornan, please understand, we have far more patients here than doctors. We are all doing the best we can."

"When can I see her?" I asked.

"When I've been informed that she's been moved to a room upstairs."

"Upstairs?"

"Yes, sir. With as severe a case hers is, there's no way your wife is going home tonight."

I fell into a chair and buried my face in my hands. "So she's going to be okay?" I asked.

"That's what we're working on now."

The nurse went to look in on a few other patients, then do some paperwork. After another agonizingly long time, she came back to inform me that Emily had been

"Where are we going?" I asked.

"Outside."

"Why?"

"So you can vent out there without causing more trouble for the others in the waiting room."

We went out to the parking lot. I followed him to the smoking area.

"What's your name?" he asked as he retrieved a pack of cigarettes from his breast pocket.

"Blake."

"I'm Mark." He shook up a cigarette and held the pack out to me. "Want one?"

"Yeah, thanks," I said.

Security Mark lit his, then mine. We stood there and smoked in the quiet for a few minutes. He finally broke the silence.

"So what's going on with you?" he asked.

I told him what had happened at home, what the EMTs said, and how we came to be at the hospital. Mark didn't say anything, he just let me talk. A couple of times he held the pack out to me again as I talked. I stopped speaking long enough to light up, then started again. By the time I had gone over every detail, I was feeling a little calmer. About that time Mark's radio squawked. A voice spoke to him in some code I didn't understand.

smoking several years before, but now I just couldn't *not* smoke. I needed something to calm my nerves. I crushed out that cigarette and went back inside. When I asked at the window, they still didn't know anything. The ER was pretty full, she said, and she didn't know when Emily was going to be seen.

"Then tell those doctors back there to get off their butts and get to work!" I yelled.

"Sir, please calm down," window-lady said. "I'm sure they're doing the best they can."

"Well, I'm not sure they are! I should have been told something by now!"

Right then one of the security guards approached me. "Sir, I need to ask you to please calm down," she said. "You're causing others to start getting more agitated than they were when they came in."

"Excuse me?" I asked. "*They're* getting more agitated? *They* are? What about my agitation? Does that not matter to you? Only theirs?"

As I stood there looking at the doors leading to the exam rooms, I saw from the corner of my eye that the first security guard had motioned another over. He touched me on the shoulder.

"Sir, come with me, please."

"What for?" I asked.

"Just come with me, please."

## The Roanoke Effect

I paused the movie and just sat and watched her instead. As time passed, her moans got louder and more frequent. All of a sudden, Emily screamed and doubled up even more than she was already.

"I'm calling 911," I said. Emily just nodded. As I waited for the ambulance to arrive, all I could do was just stand there, helpless. Her eyes were squeezed shut in agony, tears streaming down her face, while she struggled to not scream from the pain.

The ambulance arrived after what seemed like hours. They did their analysis, called it in, and loaded Emily onto the stretcher to take her to the hospital. The EMT said she was showing signs of severe food poisoning. He asked what we had for supper, so I told him. I was asked why I wasn't suffering from the same thing, and I told him I'd had a different kind of dressing on my salad. The other EMT grabbed Emily's dressing from the fridge to take and have tested.

I followed in my Bug as they had lights and siren on, going through red lights and stop signs. I was right on their bumper. There was no way I was going to stop either. As they backed in to the ambulance bay, I parked and ran inside to the window to let them know who I was and why I was there. The lady behind the glass told me they would call me when they knew something.

I went to the waiting room to sit and…well…wait. I waited, but I ended up not sitting. I paced. A lot. I grabbed a cup of that nasty waiting room coffee. I paced some more. I went outside and bummed a cigarette off the first smoker I saw. It was menthol, but I didn't care. I had quit did well. My wife, Emily, was a real estate broker/agent. With our combined incomes, we could have lived more ostentatiously if we had really wanted to. But big, fancy houses and expensive, fancy cars just weren't our style. I had a '69 VW Bug and Bus, my dream vehicles; they reminded me of my childhood. I had wanted to get a motorcycle, but my wife wasn't real thrilled with the idea. It wasn't a huge desire, so I didn't argue about it. Emily drove a late-model Chrysler 300. Nothing overly fancy, but it was reliable, and it projected the image that she knew what she was doing when it came to selling real estate.

I was sitting in my home office staring at my bookshelves when I heard Emily's car pull into the driveway. I sat there, knowing that she would come in, kiss me on the cheek, ask me about my day, and then head to the kitchen to fix supper. We always took turns, and tonight was hers. Staring at the bookshelves was what I did when trying to overcome writer's block. I had reached a critical point in the climax of my newest novel, and now had no idea how to work it out. No matter what I tried, nothing seemed to fit.

After we ate, we started watching a movie. An hour into it, Emily started holding her stomach and moaning. She then laid over on the couch and rocked herself.

"What's wrong, honey?" I asked.

"I don't know," she said. "My stomach feels like it's got a small fire building in it."

"Do you need me to take you to the ER?"

"Let's wait and see if it passes first."

## Chapter 2

All I could do while Emily slept was sit beside her bed, hold her hand, and just look at her. An hour later she was still asleep. A tech came in to check Emily's vitals and IV bag, said Hello to me, and left. Nothing else. So I went to the nurse's station to see if they could tell me when my wife might be waking up. The male nurse I asked looked at Emily's chart.

"It'll still be a while," he said. "As long as that IV bag is going, she'll be out. The sedatives are in the bag."

"It's less than half gone," I said. "How much longer will it be?"

The nurse stood up. "Let's go take a look."

## The Roanoke Effect

Back in the room, the nurse checked how much was left in the IV bag, as well as the rate of flow. "You have at least a good two hours to go. Maybe closer to three."

"Oh, wow," I said, running my fingers through my hair.

"So if you have anything to do," the nurse said, "you've got some time to do it."

I looked at his name tag. Shawn, it read. "Okay, Nurse Shawn. I'll go get a few things. I'll be back in less than an hour." I leaned down and kissed Emily on the forehead. "I'll see you soon, hon. I'll be back as quickly as I can."

Nurse Shawn walked with me as far as the nurse's station. "By the way," he added, "visiting hours will be over by the time you get back. You'll have to come in through the emergency entrance and tell security who you are."

"Thanks for the heads-up."

At the house I grabbed my laptop, a book to read, and then one for Emily in case they decided to keep her longer. I also got my journal and a couple of pens to write down any ideas I might get for the book I was currently working on, or thoughts for any future ones. Into the same bag went Emily's phone and both of our chargers. A change of clothes for the both of us, as well as the necessary toiletries. I also grabbed a coffee cup from the cabinet. I wasn't about to drink that nasty brown stuff in the waiting room. On the way back to the hospital, I stopped at 7-11 and got four large cups of the strong Brazilian blend coffee, as well as a lighter and a couple of packs of cigarettes. I could quit again, I figured, since I had done it before. Emily wouldn't like that I had started smoking again, but surely she'd understand.

Back at the hospital parking lot I looked at my watch. Ahead of schedule, actually. I had plenty of time. I burned down a couple of cigarettes in quick succession. I slung my computer bag across my torso, messenger style, grabbed my gym bag, and balanced the cardboard carry tray in my free hand. I pushed the door shut with my foot and headed for the ER door.

In the elevator, I got to thinking about our last camping trip up in the mountains. The times that we did go, which didn't seem a lot in retrospect, we always took the Bus. Because we didn't use a tent, some would call what we did "glamping." But I wouldn't call it that because we didn't use an RV. All we did was sleep in the Bus. Everything else was done at the campfire or in the woods. Emily would have preferred to rent an RV, and I wanted to use a tent. So we compromised and used the Bus instead.

I had been back in Emily's room for about an hour and a half before she started stirring. I closed my laptop and pulled my chair over beside her bed. After she was able to keep her eyes open, she saw me and smiled.

"It's you," she said in a hoarse whisper.

"Yeah, it's still me." I kissed her temple. "How are you feeling?"

"My throat feels raw and my stomach hurts," she said.

I told Emily about her stomach being pumped, her having to be knocked out for it, as the reason for her sore throat. But I wasn't sure if the pumping could cause her stomach to hurt. So I pressed the call button to tell the nurse that Emily was awake. Nurse Shawn was still on duty. He asked Emily the same thing I did, and he got the same answer as I did. Nurse Shawn listened to Emily's stomach and abdomen with his stethoscope. He frowned a little. The more he listened, the deeper his frown got.

"What's wrong?" I asked.

"I don't know," he said. "I want the on-call to listen to this." He hit a button on his in-house cell phone. "Alice. Shawn here...yeah. Page Dr. Conlon for me and have him come to four-oh-seven. Thank you."

"What did you hear?" I asked Shawn.

"I'm not sure," he said. "It might not be anything, but then again, I'm not the doctor. I want him to take a listen."

I squeezed Emily's hand reassuringly. Her brow was beginning to furrow again. Not a whole lot, but a little.

"How are you feeling now, hon?"

"My stomach is starting to hurt again, but in a different way this time. And not as bad as earlier today."

"How long will it take for the doctor to get here?" I asked Shawn.

"It all depends on where he is in the hospital, and what he might be in the middle of doing. It could be ten minutes, or it could be forty-five. You just never can tell."

It was actually only about twenty minutes before Dr. Conlon showed up, but it seemed longer. He, too, listened and pushed in different places around Emily's belly. Watching Dr. Conlon press on her abdomen took me back a few years to another doctor's office.

After Emily and I got married, we waited a couple of years to try for a family, until we were a little more settled and established. Emily took the necessary training and tests to get her realtor's license. While she learned the ins and outs of her chosen profession, I was elbows-deep with the local newspaper, learning bit by bit that real journalism had long since gone the way of the dinosaur.

We weren't high school sweethearts. We didn't even know each other until we happened to meet at an open campus college day not too far from our towns. We decided that we would much rather listen to each other than some old, dry, and dusty college professor dodder his way through a treatise on something-or-other. We exchanged phone numbers and emails. We had already become "friends" and "followers" on the various social media sites. Even though we lived less than three hours apart, I could only drive over to see her a couple of times a month. I hadn't started writing books yet. My job at the paper paid my bills with just enough extra to start saving a little.

I would go see Emily, and each time felt like I was seeing her for the first time. The twenty-five-dollar-a-night motel I checked into each trip left a lot to be desired, but it was worth it to me. It wasn't long before I proposed. I was worried that her father may not approve, as some people are of the opinion that newspaper reporters are down there with lawyers and tax collectors. But Mr. Hanson was different. He said that informing people of the news and current events, be they local, global, or somewhere in between, was a noble undertaking, and that I should be proud of my profession. We married a few months after that.

I wasn't sure then, and I'm not sure now, just exactly what my father-in-law meant, when he was talking about my job being a noble profession. It was at one time, but that was long ago. When I first started, I had visions of guys wearing fedoras with "press" papers stuck in the hat band; of smoky offices with reporters clacking away on old Royal, Smith-Corona, or Underwood typewriters, churning out Pulitzer prize-winning stories and exposés; of empty paper coffee cups and wadded-up sheets of paper; of editors barking orders to copy boys. It didn't take long to realize that those days were gone, never to be gotten back. But as much as I came to dislike my job, I stayed at it after we married until Emily started doing well and I published my first book. Like I said, No *Times* bestseller list, but my agent was good at her job, and my book, as well as those that followed, sold well.

Then we decided to start our family. After a couple of more years, nothing. As much as we enjoyed trying to begin a family, nothing was happening. So we decided to see if one or both of us had some kind of medical issue. Come to find out, Emily was barren. In her depression, my beloved wife told me to have divorce papers drawn up. She would let me go so I could have a family, even if it was with someone else.

"There is absolutely, positively, no way in this world that that is going to happen," I said. "When we got married, I vowed to you, among other things, for better or for worse. I'm not going anywhere."

Emily beat her depression by throwing herself into her work. A year later we started discussing adoption. And that was about a year prior to the Nightmare.

# Chapter 3

I was jerked back to the present when Dr. Conlon's words broke through:

"Get me an OR now," he said into his cell phone radio. "We have a problem."

Dr. Conlon glanced at me as if he was about to say something, but turned and hurried out of the room instead. Shawn was getting Emily's bed ready to roll to the elevator. A tech came in and the two of them hurried her down the hall to the waiting open doors.

"What's going on?" I called after them. I felt a hand on my shoulder. Another nurse.

"Mr. Dornan," she said, "go down to the OR waiting room. One or more of the doctors will be with you as soon as they possibly can."

"But what's going on?" I repeated.

"I don't know," the nurse said. "I wasn't told."

I didn't even go back to Emily's room for anything before heading back down. More pacing. I desperately wanted a cigarette, but I didn't dare leave, not even for a minute. The minutes stretched into what seemed like hours. Every time I heard a door open I expected, I hoped, that it was Dr. Conlon or the surgeon coming to tell me that my Emily was just fine. Finally someone in surgical scrubs and cap came out. But he didn't act as if he were bringing good news.

"No," I said. "No. No. No." I couldn't stop repeating it. It was like a stylus skipping on the same word over and over.

"I'm sorry, Mr. Dornan," the surgeon said. "We did all we could. There was a perforation in the lining of your wife's stomach. It may have happened when her stomach was pumped earlier this morning, but we don't know for sure."

I was trying to process what he was saying, but I couldn't keep up. Suddenly my legs gave out and I fell back into my chair.

"We tried repairing the perforation," he was saying, "but we were too late. Your wife hemorrhaged to death. I'm sorry."

## The Roanoke Effect

I leapt to my feet with newfound strength and grabbed the surgeon by his scrub shirt. "Get back in there and save my wife!" I screamed in his face. "Do your job and save her!"

He tried prying my fingers loose. No use. I wasn't about to let go.

"Mr. Dornan!" he yelled back at me. "Get ahold of yourself!" He grabbed my wrists. "Your wife is gone. I'm sorry, but there's nothing else we can do."

At that point I lost any other shred of composure I may have been holding on to. I began yelling and screaming uncontrollably. I felt myself grabbed from behind, and then falling to the floor. A sharp sting in my arm. Sounds of people talking as if behind a waterfall. Then blackness.

# Chapter 4

I opened my eyes and blinked at the bright lights. I tried to shield my eyes, but my arms wouldn't move. I looked down, and my wrists had leather straps buckled around them, and secured to the bed railing. Dr. Conlon was sitting by the door.

"I was beginning to think we had given you too much," he said.

"Too much what?" I asked.

"Knockout drugs, if you want to call it that. The amount a man of your size calls for didn't even faze you. You were completely out of control. We gave you enough Thorazine to knock out a gorilla." The doctor got up and walked over to me. He tapped the leather straps with his finger. "You're restrained for everyone's safety, yours and ours both."

"What happened?" I asked.

"What do you remember?" he countered.

I closed my eyes. "I remember the surgeon telling me that my wife was dead..."

"I'm sure he didn't put it like that," Dr. Conlon interrupted.

"No, but it's the same thing."

"Then what?" he asked. "What do you remember next?"

"I kind of remember grabbing the front of his shirt. After that, the next thig I know, I'm strapped down like Frankenstein's monster."

"Like I said, it's for all our safety." Dr. Conlon looked at my face and in my eyes, as if to read my mind. He continued. "Dr. Carvin doesn't want to press any assault charges. He knows that some news is very difficult, even impossible at times, to process. Today wasn't the first time someone tried to shoot the messenger, so to speak."

"I am really sorry about that," I said. "I'll tell him, too, if he's around."

"I will pass the message on to him," Dr. Conlon said. "He's doing up his reports right now." He began to unbuckle the straps on my wrists.

"What about all my...?" I began.

"Your things are all in the closet over there," Dr. Conlon said, jerking his head toward the other side of the room. "No need for you to go back upstairs."

"Thank you," I said. "I was really not looking forward to it. At all."

Dr. Conlon lowered the bed rail. I swung my feet to the floor and stood up. And immediately sat back right down as the room began spinning.

"Stay there," Dr. Conlon said. "I'll get your things."

He brought my bags over and set them on the adjustable table by the bed. "The coffee got tossed," he said.

"I don't care," I mumbled. I dug my phone out. "I've got some calls to make."

"I'll leave you alone now," Dr. Conlon said, "but you're not going to be driving anywhere for a while. I'll have some water and coffee sent in for you."

"Thank you, Doctor," I said. "I appreciate it."

After he was gone, I made the excruciating calls to my parents and in-laws. After the calls were done, I buried my face in a pillow and poured out my broken heart, in the form of hot tears. After I cried myself out, I got up. I washed my face, drank a glass of water, and composed myself. I slipped my cigarettes and lighter into my pocket, grabbed the now-tepid coffee Dr. Conlon had delivered, and went to the nurse's station.

## The Roanoke Effect

"If you would, please," I said, "tell Dr. Conlon that I'm going outside for a little bit. I'm not leaving, just going outside."

The nurse said she'd pass along the message. Going through the ER waiting room, I made a detour by the coffee machine. It wasn't good, but it was hot, and would heat up what I already had. The smoking area had a picnic table, so I headed there. The only light around came from the parking lot lamps, since it was after three in the morning. I had been out for several hours. There was nobody else around, for which I was grateful. I drank my coffee and smoked in silence, listening to the night sounds: cicadas and crickets, tires on pavement as traffic drove by, the drone of various AC units running. I really didn't know how much time had passed, nor did I care. I was just glad that no one was trying to console me. With the mood I was in, I would have wanted to punch anyone who tried. I wouldn't have actually done it, maybe, but I would have wanted to. I stretched the coffee out until my cigarette pack was empty.

I went back inside to look for Dr. Conlon. I was told he had left already. My intention was to have him take a look at me to determine if I was okay to drive, but now I no longer cared. I collected my things and left. As I started the Bug, my stomach churned and growled. Although I in no way felt the least bit hungry, I knew I needed something in my stomach besides coffee and water. On my way home I stopped at the same 7-11. I got a coffee, a two-pack of frozen breakfast burritos, and another pack of cigarettes. After paying, I nuked the burritos for a couple of minutes and ate them on the way home. They were tasteless to me, but I knew I needed something.

## David Nelson

    At home I sat in my car, windows down, smoking and drinking my coffee, staring at my empty house. I sat there until the black sky started getting lighter in the east. I absolutely did not want to go inside. But at the same time, I knew that I needed to. I plodded on leaden feet to the front door, and was loathe to unlock it. I finally forced myself to, and then just stood just inside the doorway, not moving. I somehow managed to close the door behind me and make it to the couch. No way was I going to our bedroom. I lay down on the couch and cried myself to sleep.

# Chapter 5

All the next week I was completely on autopilot. I had arrangements to make, and I forced myself to maintain control. I didn't have to cook anything due to well-wishers bringing me all kinds of food. All I had to do was heat it up. If I even felt like it. I didn't eat a whole lot, mostly just slept. I took a lot of sleep aids that week because they helped me sleep without dreaming.

I don't remember a whole lot about Emily's funeral. I remember seeing a lot of people, smelling a lot of flowers, and shaking a lot of hands. I managed to mumble something that resembled "Thank you" more times than I can remember. And then they were gone.

It took a couple of days, but reality finally set in. I couldn't do anything for a long time, including eating. I forced myself to eat a little of the leftovers in the fridge. I went to the liquor store around the corner and down the street a couple of blocks. I got two fifths of bourbon, a three-liter of Coke, and a carton of peach flavored little cigars later, I headed back home. The next few days were spent on the couch smoking, drinking, and eating junk food. I got off the couch long enough to go to the bathroom. No showers. No shaves. No haircuts. I slept, or passed out, where I sat.

Life no longer held any meaning for me. I quit writing. I quit reading. I quit learning my guitar. I happened to empty my mailbox one day coming back from the liquor store because it was crammed full. I dropped the mail inside the front door and left it there. No TV, no movies, no radio. The only reason bills got paid was because they were on auto-pay at our bank. My phone went dead because I never plugged it in. I was actually glad though; I hated the sound of it ringing. At one point I plugged it in long enough to call my parents and in-laws to let them know I was still alive. Then I let it die again.

I had no idea how much time passed, and again, I didn't care. I didn't care about anything. All I knew one day was that I was out of whiskey, out of little cigars, and I stunk so bad that I couldn't stand to smell myself. After a very long and hot shower, I put on clean clothes and threw the others in the dumpster in the alley behind our house. Same with the moldy leftovers in the fridge. Again, phone charged enough to make a few calls to people to come get their dishes off my front porch. Then back to the liquor store for twice as much booze, smokes, and junk food as before.

# Chapter 6

Now the Nightmare has begun. Not a nightmare of zombies, vampires, or werewolves. At least with those I could have fought back. Or at least tried. When I woke up, I saw three empty bottles on the floor. I still had one more, but wanted to replenish my stock before I ran out again. I didn't trust myself to keep my Bug between the curbs, so I walked instead. I didn't really notice anything until I got to the store. I grabbed what I wanted and went to the counter to check out. That's when it hit me.

There was no one else in the store. Not behind the counter, not in the back rooms, no one. I did my own transaction. I swiped my card, tapped in my PIN, tore off the receipt, and left. On my way back to the house, I stopped to open one of the bottles. I downed three gulps of Jack in quick succession. I had been getting more used to drinking it straight, but mostly out of laziness. I just didn't want to expend the effort of pouring the whiskey and then the Coke into a glass. Why do that? I thought. It's quicker to drink straight from the bottle. The quick chug I did burned all the way down and threw me into a coughing fit. I wasn't *that* used to it. After I caught my breath and wiped my eyes, I started off again. No more than five steps before I suddenly stopped, the bags swinging in m y hands. I looked around. I saw nobody.

    Not.

    One.

    Single.

    Soul.

    I was completely, totally, utterly alone. No sounds of kids playing. No cars driving down the streets. Nothing. Just me. My nightmare had truly begun.

# Chapter 7

    I drove all over town. I could not believe what I was seeing. Or rather, not seeing. While I saw some dogs, cats, and the usual birds and squirrels, I saw not one single person. There were no crashed vehicles anywhere, nothing that looked like anyone had left in a hurry. Everything was neat and tidy. Mostly. Leaves danced across lawns, driveways, and streets. Cars were parked at banks, grocery stores, and other places of business. Residential areas looked almost like something out of *Leave it to Beaver*.

    It's not like it was flawless or unblemished. There were oil stains in driveways, cracks in sidewalks, and little chunks of pavement missing from streets here and there. I was very hesitant to go inside any of the houses. I expected everyone to come back. I had gone up to several of them and knocked or rang the doorbell, all to no avail. What response I did get was dogs barking, cats jumping up on the window sill, or birds singing, chirping, or whistling inside.

I hoped that I was just dreaming, that when I awoke the next morning everybody would be back. Including Emily. Such was not the case. I tried calling my parents, but the call dropped without even ringing. Same with my in-laws. Emily and I were each an only child, so there were no siblings to contact. Then I tried the time and temp number at the bank. That one worked. The machine answered, and I was informed that it was now eleven twenty-seven am, seventy-six degrees, and first-time homeowners could get a loan at one-point-nine percent for the first twelve months, increasing to two-point-four-seven after that.

I could not wrap my brain around the fact that I was, for all intents and purposes, the last person on earth. I saw no evidence to the contrary.

But something else puzzled me. There was still electricity, there was still water, and presumably, there was still natural gas flowing to all the places they had been before. All I could think was that everything nowadays was fully automated and self-contained, needing almost no human intervention. Kind of spooky, actually, to think that computers could do all that by themselves. Reminded me of a movie about a computer rebelling against its maker and building an army of killer cyborgs. Fun thoughts. But what if something happened and it all went down? What then? Who was going to fix it?

The gas gauge on my Bug was showing less than a quarter tank after driving around town. I pulled into the next gas station. The high price for premium made no difference now. It was free. Or it would be as long as I could figure out how to turn the pumps on.

I did get them turned on and filled up. I drove home and got the Bus and went back to the same station for another fill-up. I couldn't bring myself, though, to even sit in Emily's car, let alone drive it right now.

I decided that it might be a good idea to start eating real food again. I pulled a steak from the freezer. It had been there since before Emily died, but as I always did, it was vacuum-sealed. As it thudded on the counter, I suddenly began to wonder about the meats and produce in the various grocery stores around town. I went to the first one I thought of, the one nearest our house. Sure enough, the refrigerated meat bins were pretty full. I used a shopping cart to transfer all the meats to the store's industrial-size freezer for safer keeping. It took several trips, but I got it done. I left everything in the freezer bins out on the floor for the time being. The steak from the freezer at home would take a while to thaw, so I took the time to go to three more stores before heading back to the house. I decided to take a couple of roasts with me for the Crock Pot, a beef sirloin tip and a Boston Butt. I figured there probably wasn't much of anything I could do about the fresh produce in the stores.

At home I put the beef roast in the freezer, and the Boston Butt in the fridge. It was going in the Crock Pot the next day. I put the steak in a skillet with a little bit of oil, and heated a can of green beans.

I ate in silence.

I almost didn't finish, but I also knew that this wasn't the time for me to give up. Emily would want me to go on. After eating, I took the Bus to the liquor store and got all the empty boxes I could find. The racks inside the doors still had newspapers in them. The *Daily Town Cryer* brought a sad smile to my face. It was the paper I was working at when Emily and I met. I got home and began wrapping and boxing up almost all the dishes. I kept out very few. One each of plate, bowl, drinking glass, and coffee cup. One set of silverware plus steak knife. One skillet, one sauce pan, one stew/chili pot. Kitchen knife set, ladle, spatula, egg turner, and two big serving spoons, one slotted and one not. Two wooden stirring spoons. Crock Pot and a couple of platters. If I decided that I needed anything else, I'd just have to dig it out of the garage. I took a smoke break and had a drink. One of each turned into several.

I jumped up off the couch, dropped my glass, and spilled the ashtray. All the exertion of that day had worn me out. That and the alcohol put me to sleep before I knew it. My cigarette burning down to my fingers was what woke me up. I cleaned up the mess, changed into a pair of shorts. I had one last drink and smoke before going back to sleep. On purpose this time.

# Chapter 8

It's been a week now since everybody disappeared. I spent the last several days going to the different grocery stores to put the meats in the freezers. At some point along the way, I got the bright idea to try dehydrating some fruits and vegetables.

I had also gotten to thinking about our neighbors, the Brauners. They had two Rottweilers, George and Gracie. They were normally very gentle and friendly, but I was worried that they might not be so much now, after possibly not having anything to eat or drink for a few days. I carried a fifteen-pound bag of Gravy Train to the front door. I tore the top completely off before knocking. The house seemed to shake as the Rotts began barking. I had to wait for a break in the noise before calling their names.

"George!" I shouted. "Gracie!"

The barking immediately turned to whining. I tried the knob. It was unlocked. I pushed the door open just far enough to get the bag of food in. I made sure that it fell over and spilled. As the nuggets scattered across the floor, George and Gracie were jumping over each other getting to the food. I stood there and watched them eat. If they'd had tails, they would have been black and brown blurs. As it was, their backsides were doing all the moving. Every so often they would look up from the food pile and glance my direction. I had always liked the dogs, so I decided that I would take them home with me.

While I was pragmatic enough to know that I could not possibly save all the pets in town, I wanted to try and save as many as I could. I started with my neighborhood first, and worked my way out from there. At first I used the Bus to haul bags of dog and cat food, but soon switched to something else. I decided that I needed a pickup for what I was doing. I was definitely able to carry much more at one time. The dealership owner certainly wasn't going to miss the truck.

I approached each house the same. I knocked on the door first. If there was no sound from inside I went around to the back yard fence. If I got no response there either, I spray-painted an "X" on the front door. I also watched the front windows for any cats.

Houses with dogs or cats inside got a "D" or "C" spray-painted on the door. If there were both, then both letters were left. Dogs inside got an open bag thrown in and the door quickly shut. Cats inside got an open bag thrown in, but the front door and storm door or screens were left open. Houses with both got the dog food first. I waited a couple of minutes to make sure the dogs were good and occupied before putting in the cat food. Then I closed the door again. The back yards that had dogs got an open bag on the side of the house with no gate. While the dog, or dogs, were busy eating, I went to the other side and opened the gate. I didn't want them trapped with nowhere to go. Same with the inside dogs. While they ate near the front door, I snuck around back and opened the back door and gate. A large number of these dogs and cats most likely would not survive, but they would at least have a chance, and not die alone, all cooped up. I was just glad that there wasn't a zoo in town.

A couple of strange things I noticed: each house I went to, the doors were all unlocked. And all the dogs that did seem a little vicious acted more interested in getting away than attacking me. I thought that very odd.

Quite a few of the dogs, and even a couple of the cats, wanted to follow me around all the time. But so far George and Gracie were the only pets inside my house. I had decided to go jogging on occasion, and when I did, the Rotts went with me. And when they did, most of the other dogs stayed away, but a few went with us. After a couple of weeks of feeding and releasing pets, I figured that if I hadn't gotten to them by that point, it was already too late. It saddened me to think I had missed any, but I also had a small comfort knowing that I had saved as many as I had. It did help.

# Chapter 9

    Although I still imbibed, it had been a while since I drank myself to sleep. And it was going to be a while before I went through everything from that store near me. I had started trading off between those little cigars and regular cigarettes to make the former last a little longer. Those little cigars aren't actually cigars. They look like cigarettes, except they're wrapped in brown paper instead of white. Plus they come in different flavors. Even the plain ones tasted and smelled a lot different from cigarettes. And better.

    With George and Gracie living with me, the house began to feel crowded. So I decided to go house hunting. I knew the area that I wanted to look, I just didn't know which house I was going to want. I loaded the dogs up into the Bus and took off. After a couple of hours, I finally decided on a two-and-a-half story Victorian surrounded by what looked like a ten-foot brick wall with a wood and wrought-iron gate. And the gate stood wide open.

Strange.

Inside the house I found two remotes for the gate sitting on the counter by the door leading to the garage. There was a gun cabinet in what I presumed was a study. Inside were three rifles, two shotguns, and four handguns. Several boxes of ammunition for each. Although I had never owned any firearms, I had shot several over the years. So I wasn't a complete stranger to them. In the bottom section of the cabinet was a holster and gunbelt, the kind you see in the western movies: loops full of bullets, maybe a few missing, six-shooter riding low and tied down. The revolver in the cabinet was a Ruger .44. At least that's what was stamped on the barrel. It fit the holster like they were made for each other. I buckled the gunbelt around my hips like I'd seen in the movies. It felt good. The added weight of the gun was somehow reassuring to me. I checked the two lever-action rifles. One was a .30-.30, the other was a Henry .44, same caliber as the Ruger. For some reason I loaded the Henry and took it with me. The Ruger was already loaded.

In the Bus I laid the rifle on the floor beside me, barrel pointing forward. I would rather a bullet accidentally go through the engine than one of the dogs. The holster was a right-hand draw, but I was also wanting one for the left. I had discovered one time that I was ambidextrous with a handgun. But I was also thinking that a left-handed gunbelt would make me feel more balanced. And I had always liked the old west anyway.

But first things first. Back at our house I got the pickup and went to the U-Haul yard to get a car dolly. With that I got the Bug, Bus, and Chrysler to my new house. I said earlier that our house had started feeling crowded with the two Rotts living there. And while that's true, it wasn't the only, or even main, reason I moved out. The memories were too painful; Emily was everywhere I looked. Maybe someday I would go back. I just couldn't stay there anymore right now.

I left the Rotts at Victoria (that's what I decided to call my new place; I know, it's not very original; don't judge), and took the Bus back to our house to get what things I wanted with me. The few kitchen things I mentioned before, my laptop, our phones (simply for photos; it's not like I could use them for anything else), the fifty or so DVDs we had, our picture album, and a studio portrait of the two of us. I know that last part sounds kind of contradictory, or even counterintuitive to my reasons for moving out, but when you lose somebody like that, you don't just "get over it." If it got to be too much, I could always put those things away for a while. "Victoria" would be a buffer for me. Living in our old house had Emily everywhere. I couldn't handle it anymore. So while taking those few things sounds like I was defeating my own purpose, I really wasn't. It takes losing someone like that to really understand.

I loaded everything into the Bus. I had no pet carriers, so the two cats rode uncaged. They had been hanging around the house since I had liberated them, and went with the Rotts and me on our walks and runs. Both males, I named the grey tabby O'Malley, and the solid yellow one Chauncey. They rode well, no fuss. They both stood on the front passenger seat, forepaws on the dash, just watching as we drove. I tapped the remote as I turned up the new street. The Victorian wasn't too far from the corner, so I timed it well. The gate finished opening just as I got to the driveway. I tapped the remote again, but the gates moved slow enough that I had ample time and room to drive through without any problems.

After I fed and watered the animals, I made the necessary trips to carry everything in. The dogs ran around outside in the huge yard while the cats explored their new home. I didn't bother putting anything but the food away. Well, cold stuff anyway. I just put the boxes of nonperishables on the living room floor for the time being.

Out in the yard I found the Rotts laying under the big magnolia tree, panting, their tongues lolling out.

"You two want to go shopping?" I asked them.

They jumped up and ran over to me, their stubby tails trying to wag.

"I'll take that for a Yes," I said. "Come on."

I opened the driver's door of the pickup and they jumped right in, one on the front passenger seat, the other in the back. I drove to the same dealership I had gotten the truck from. In the office I found keys for several cargo vans. I was thinking I would need more space than the pickup had. Outside I made an exaggerated show of trying to decide which white cargo van I wanted. I looked back at the Rotts, and they just sat there, ears perked, heads cocked to one side. They looked pretty comical like that. I even chuckled a little. I think it's the first time I even cracked a smile since...since Emily.

I actually knew which van, naturally, because I had only one set of keys. But it was kind of liberating to act a little goofy. It even felt good. A little. I let the dogs out of the pickup and opened the side door of the van. The Rotts jumped in and lay down. I just climbed in after them and shut the door behind me rather than walk around to get in. I buckled the seatbelt and started the engine. I waited for all the gauges to come up: gas tank was half full. I put the van in gear, and then looked back at the Rotts.

"Traffic's gonna be a little light today," I said.

They did a growl/moan and laid their heads down. The stoplights were still on their green-yellow-red cycles, but there was obviously no need to stop for a red. But then I did. A dog chased a squirrel out into the street, right in front of me. I slammed on the brakes, and over the screeching tires I could hear the dog's claws skittering on the van floor. Both dog and squirrel made it across safely, and I was suddenly glad I was still in the habit of wearing a seatbelt. Even though I was the only driver around, I was going to have to watch out for other animals. I had been doing about fifty down the main street through town, but I kept it at forty now.

At the Superstore I went to the stockroom and got a flatcart. I loaded up every case of half-pint, pint, and quart

# The Roanoke Effect

canning jars that I could find. I wasn't going to be doing any canning, I just wanted them to put the dehydrated fruits and veggies in. Every lid and ring went too. On my way to the van I got a vacuum sealer for jars. Then, almost as an afterthought, I grabbed one for bags. Plus all the bag material. Because you just never know.

I stacked all the cases of jars about midway between the front seats and back doors. I had left the Henry back at Victoria, mainly because I didn't have any kind of rack or clamp to keep it in. And I didn't want it getting scratched up on the van floor. But I still wore the Ruger. Back inside I went. In the pet department I loaded up with bags of dog and cat food. I threw in several boxes of cans for both as well. Two litter boxes and a few bags of clumping litter. Some species-specific toys. Food and water dishes for the cats. From automotive I got a large oil drain pan to feed the dogs in. Lawn and garden gave me some twenty-gallon buckets for outside water, 3 and ½ gallon for inside. I was going to need some clothes, but at the moment I didn't have the time to try any on. I figured that since the cats had eaten, they would soon be needing the use of the boxes and litter. So I just grabbed a pair of shorts and packages of socks, t-shirts, and undies of the shelf on my way out. In the van, I stacked the bags of pet food in front of and behind the canning jars. I packed them in as best I could, hoping I wouldn't have any broken ones when I got back to Victoria. With everything, loaded in the van, the only places for the dogs were between the seats, or on the passenger seat, as more stuff had gone on the floor in front of it. I drove back to the house even slower because of the jars.

## David Nelson

By the time I got everything unloaded from the van, I was worn out. I hadn't taken any kind of meat out of the freezer, and nothing else that I had looked good to me. So I hopped in the Bus and drove to the nearest convenience store. There were eleven cans of ravioli left on the shelf. I double-bagged them all. Plus a two-liter bottle of off-brand cola and a pint of bourbon from behind the counter. And some more smokes, matches, and lighters.

At Victoria I showered before I did anything else. I just knew that after I sat down on the VERY comfortable couch, I most likely wouldn't want to get up again. Before going inside, I had put the extra security bar across the double gate. For some reason I felt better about it. I dumped four cans of ravioli into the saucepan to heat. While that was going, I measured four cups of the new cola into an empty tea jug. Then I added a half-cup of bourbon. Stirred and put it in the freezer for quick chill. Having it pre-mixed would save me time. But then again, it wasn't like I had lots of other things to do, places to go, or people to see crowding my schedule.

With the ravioli heated and a movie in the Blu-ray player, I plopped onto the middle of the couch and put my feet up on the coffee table. I had George and Gracie sitting one on either side of me, and the cats had settled down on the arms, one at each end. I waited through the anti-piracy and home-viewing-only screens before I started eating. I didn't want to finish my meal, such that it was, before the movie even started. A retired assassin returning because his muscle car is stolen and his dog is killed made for an interesting movie. Paused it twice: once for a ravioli refill and again for bathroom break followed by a drink and smokes.

After the movie was over, I made sure doors and windows were locked, then went to bed. The master bedroom was on the second floor, and had a California king. I was asleep almost as soon as my head hit the pillow. Maybe even before.

# Chapter 10

When I woke up, George and Gracie were both stretched out on the bed. They waited there while I got up and went through my morning routine. It seems like the only time they ever let me out of their sight was when they were out in the yard and I was inside. In the house at least one of them followed me around, but usually both. When we went to any stores, they both stayed right with me. As if protecting me.

There are times, when I am going through my day that memories of things my parents or in-laws said to me come to mind. And the memories are so vivid that it's almost like they're here with me. But that's obviously not the case.

## The Roanoke Effect

I decided this day to stay in and so some slicing, dicing, and dehydrating for a change. I took the sirloin tip roast and a package of pork chops out of the freezer. The roast went into the fridge, and the chops went into the sink. Chops for supper tonight, roast in the Crock-Pot tomorrow.

I have no idea how many pounds of onions, bell peppers, carrots, and potatoes I chopped and/or sliced for the dehydrator. What I do know is that I rubbed a couple of blisters on my cutting hand, and cut myself several times on the other. I had four dehydrators at the house, with eight to twelve trays in each one. I did up enough veggies to fill them all. No less than ten hours before they would be ready. I thought about getting more done so they would be ready to go, but my hands said no. So instead I put the triple antibiotic ointment on my cuts and re-bandaged them, and wrapped my blistered hand with gauze and waited for them to pop.

I made some tea and spent the rest of the afternoon sitting outside in the shade, drinking iced tea and watching the dogs and cats do their thing. Or I'd watch the birds flitting from tree to tree, and listen to them chirp and sing. Squirrels would show off their acrobatic skills, as they too, jumped from tree to tree, or scampered along the top of the wall. At one point a squirrel scolded George for something. What, I wasn't quite sure. Getting too close, I suppose. And because I wasn't occupied doing something, my mind drifted back to Emily and our life together.


I had rented us a cabin up in the mountains for our first anniversary. The plan was for her to take off work at lunch time, and we would leave when she got home. The Bus was already loaded. But Emily was later getting home than I expected. I was getting really worried when my cell phone rang. It was Emily.

"Are you okay?" I asked by way of answering.

"Yes, honey, I'm fine," she said. "I had an errand to run before I came home, but it took longer than I thought it would. I'll be home in a few minutes."

"Okay," I said, relieved. "Please be careful. I love you."

"Love you, too. See you in a bit."

Sure enough, Emily pulled into the driveway less than five minutes later. I went out to see if there was anything I needed to carry in. She said that, yes, actually, there was. She took my hand and led me to the rear of the car.

"Close your eyes," Emily said.

"Do what?"

"Close your eyes," she repeated.

"As you wish," I said, and closed them.

I heard the trunk release. "Keep them closed," Emily said. Then I heard the slight creak of the hinges as the trunk was opened all the way.

"Now open them."

## The Roanoke Effect

I did. And I couldn't believe what I was seeing. Sitting right in the middle of the trunk, on top of the spare tire cavity, was an antique Royal typewriter. I stepped closer to get a better look.

"It's from 1930," she said. "Do you like it?' She almost sounded nervous.

"Do I like it?" I asked. "Are you kidding? I love it!" I swept her up in my arms and swung her around. "Thank you, hon. It's wonderful."

"I was hoping you'd like it," she said.

"I really do."

"Good. Now I need you to carry it into the house. That thing weighs a ton!"


I was brought back to the present by the Rotts barking. They were staring at the gates. I followed their gaze but saw nothing. Even after they stopped barking, George and Gracie continued staring at the double gate. I dismissed it as probably squirrels, or maybe a cat. Other dogs would have barked in return, most likely, because they had before.

I went inside to grab the other tea pitcher and use the bathroom. On the way back out the door I grabbed another pack of smokes. I poured a glass of tea, lit a cigarette, and settled back into my chair. All of a sudden, a memory of my mother talking to me came to mind.

"We love you, Blake," she said, "no matter what. Never forget that."

What brought that memory to mind, I couldn't say. But it brought tears to my eyes to think about it. I set my tea glass down and looked over at the dogs.

"You know what?" They perked their ears up. "I need something stronger than this tea. These memories are about to do me in."

When I stood up, Gracie got up, too. George stayed where he was, but watched intently.

"Chauncey!" I hollered. "O'Malley! C'mon!"

I heard the scritchity-scratch of claws on bark as the cats climbed down out of the magnolia tree. I opened the door and they ran inside. Gracie followed me in. I got the cola/bourbon jug out of the fridge. It was nice and cold. And had plenty of room for another mix. So I measured another four cups of cola and a full cup of bourbon this time. I poured the whiskey in, followed by the cola and gave it a good stir. Back outside I forced myself to think about what I should do in the next few days rather than what had happened in the past. I sat for a couple of more hours, smoking and drinking. It was all I could do to keep from breaking down. George and Gracie had come over and lay down by me, one on either side. They apparently could sense my grief. I finally got up and went back inside. I poured a couple of fingers into my glass before putting the pitcher back into the fridge. I checked the dehydrators. They were done so I turned them off. I would take care of the contents tomorrow. One more smoke with that last glass, then off to bed.

    I don't know how much more I can take.

## Chapter 11

The contents of the dehydrators took up surprisingly little room. A less than I imagined. So I divvied them up into jars, sealed them, and set them aside. I really wasn't looking forward to all that slicing and chopping so soon. Then I remembered a video I had seen on line by a lady that bought frozen vegetables specifically to dehydrate. I seemed to remember her saying that four-pound bag dehydrated would fit into a quart jar, maybe even a pint. I would just have to try it and see.

I went back to the same Superstore with the Rotts in tow. I got separate bags of corn, carrots, peas, and green beans, as well as several various mixes. I let several of the bags sit out to thaw while the rest went into the freezer. While the veggies thawed for a bit, I took four aspirin for my

# The Roanoke Effect

headache. My stomach didn't feel all that great either; I had forgotten to eat last night. Not a good idea.

"Why didn't you guys remind me about supper?" I asked the Rotts. They just sat and looked at me. "I guess it's chops tonight and roast tomorrow, them."

I let the dogs out to run around while I filled the dehydrator trays again. My hands thanked me for not cutting anything that time. Ten to twelve hours and they should be done. After I made sure they were all going, I let the dogs back in. I replenished all food and water.

"I'm going back to bed for a while," I told the animals. "Please don't call me for anything." Chauncey and O'Malley just looked at me. George and Gracie followed me upstairs, as always.

Sometime later (I don't know how long), I was awaked by the dogs growling and huffing.

"What's going on?" I asked them, rubbing my eyes.

George jumped off the bed and stood at the door growling. His hackles were up. I had never seen him like that. Gracie was growling, too. Then suddenly a metallic sound outside. George started scratching at the bedroom door. I opened up the door and the Rotts bolted to the staircase. I followed. Halfway down, I turned and ran back up to the bedroom. I grabbed my gun belt and ran back down the stairs. At the landing I glanced out the window and stopped dead in my tracks.

The gates were moving.

The dogs were at the front door, whining and barking, scratching and digging, trying to get out. I got the door open as fast as I could. As soon as the door and screen were open, the Rotts ran toward the gates. They moved very little now, as if they were just settling back on their hinges. I had a hard time seeing in the sudden brightness, and I didn't have any sunglasses. I ran barefoot to the gate, gun belt in hand. I quickly swung the belt around my hips and buckled it, all-the-while listening intently. I slid the .44 out of the holster as quietly as I could.

I listened some more.

Hands on the dogs' heads to keep them quiet.

I heard nothing else. Gingerly I climbed up the inside of the gate and slowly peered over the top. I looked left, then right.

Nothing.

Absolutely nothing in sight. Not one dog. Not one cat. Not even a squirrel.

Strange indeed.

# Chapter 12

The dehydrators were far from done, but I couldn't get back to sleep for thinking about the gate incident. I was beyond puzzled. It was more like baffled. And before I knew it I was trying to figure out the philosophical differences between a puzzle and a baffle, and how they differed from a confuse and a bewilder.

My brain got to hurting from trying to figure it all out. So I quit and decided to clean the rifles, shotguns and hand guns. I took my time, making sure I cleaned each part as best I could. Well, except the Glock .40 and the Kimber .45. I had no idea how to take them apart. Maybe the police or sheriff's stations would have some manuals on them. If not, I'd have to stick with revolvers and single-shots. And speaking of single-shots, after I did what gun cleaning I could, I took a single shot of my CW (cola/whiskey) and went back to bed for a couple of more hours, finally able to sleep again.

I didn't want to sleep too long because I wanted to keep some semblance of a schedule. I figured that the best way to get completely discombobulated is to let everything descend into total chaos. Not something I wanted to experience. I'd had enough already.

I remembered to eat supper this time. I fried the pork chops but didn't bother with breading them first. Just heated some oil in the skillet and put the chops in. I also mixed up some instant mashed potatoes with sour cream and garlic powder, and made gravy from the pork chop drippings. A bag of corn was heated and mixed in with the potatoes. I always did like mixing my corn, peas or mixed veggies in with my mashed potatoes. By the time I finished eating, put the leftovers in the fridge and washed and put away the few dishes, the dehydrators were just about done. I counted out the number of trays that had been four pounds of frozen mixed vegetables. They pretty much filled a quart jar. The full jars of dried corn, peas, carrots, green beans and such were filled "like kind with like kind." Afterward I made half a pot of coffee, watched a movie, and went to bed.

I had no more incidents with the gate.

# Chapter 13

Breakfast consisted of three fried eggs, a reheated pork chop, and some coffee. I never had been one to drink a lot of the stuff, or even on any kind of regular basis, but I decided that I was beginning to really like it. And being the relative newbie, I hadn't built up to plain black yet. My taste buds were still sissified enough to want cream and sugar. I decided that my next grocery trip would include various flavors and strengths of coffees, as well different non-dairy creamers. All the milk, cream, and half-and-half had long since gone bad. I got a gallon jug of milk three weeks into the Nightmare, and it had far surpassed its expiration date. I went to all the stores I found that sold milk, and had to dump it all. So from that point on, it was powdered or canned milk all the way. Not the greatest stuff in the world, but it worked for cooking. I just had to remember to make sure to mix the powdered milk REALLY well. The steel whisk worked best for that.

The Rotts rode in the back of the cargo van again, but I didn't think they much cared for it. On the way to the Superstore, I detoured by a carpet shop. I cut a 6-by-10-foot piece inside, then trimmed it down once I got it in the van. George and Gracie acted a lot happier with that thick pile under them.

On to the store.

Coffees and creamers, both liquid and powder, went into the basket. Two cases each of chili, ravioli, stew and clam chowder. I wanted something quick and easy for times I didn't feel like actually cooking anything.

After all that was loaded into the van, I went back to the sporting goods section. I got all the rifles and shotguns they had (which was a grand total of 53) and all the ammunition. The guns in the display racks I put in padded cases. Those still boxed in the back just stayed in the boxes.

Driving back to the house I stopped by the police department. Nothing untoward there, unless you count the complete absence of human life other than myself. As I'd hoped I did find several manuals on field stripping various models of auto and semi-auto rifles, shotguns, and hand guns. At the sheriff's office though, things were a little different. The wind had kicked up at some point, and one of the glass front doors kept moving on its hinges. With my right hand on the butt of my Ruger, I slowly pushed the door open with my left. Leaves and dirt had been blown inside back who knew when. A couple of the fluorescent bulbs flickered. It was not just a little eerie. I walked slowly through the main reception area. The Rotts followed close behind, making no noise on the thin office carpet. I kept looking around, half expecting someone to appear at any moment. I pushed open a door leading toward the back of the building, toward the jail cells. I stepped into the hallway and heard several loud clicks. I about jumped out of my skin as I spun around drawing my gun halfway from the holster. Then it dawned on me. I looked down at the dogs.

"Remind me to trim your nails soon, okay? Stop scaring me like that."

I resumed my slow walk down the hallway, the dogs click-click-clicking behind me. I rounded a corner and was greeted by loud hissing and a mouth full of sharp teeth. Even George and Gracie were startled. The hissing continued as a mother opossum shielded her young from the sudden intruders. I decided then and there that I would come back and get everything usable, then prop all the doors open, especially the cell doors. While most of the towns' inhabitants could fit through the bars, there would be some that couldn't. My search of that building turned up a few more firearm manuals that I didn't have already. On my way back out, I propped the hall and front doors open. As I backed the van out of the parking space, something else occurred to me: the gun cages at the police department and the sheriff's office were both unlocked.

Things were getting curiouser and curiouser.

## Chapter 14

With the rifles and shotguns brought back from the Superstore, I filled the gun cabinet in the study. I was also going to have to start bringing back more cabinets and maybe a wall-mount rifle rack or three. Every long gun in the cabinet was loaded. The Henry I kept with me, taking it outside, inside, upstairs and down. Also in the study, I cleared the books from a few of the shelves to stack all the boxes of ammunition. The unopen cases were stacked on the floor. Hunting and pocket knives were going to be the next things I got from the Superstore. I might even grab some pellet and BB guns just for fun.

Earlier I had dumped the contents of one of the stew cans into a bowl and nuked it for a quick lunch. But a few hours later, after I had finished separating the ammo by caliber and gauge, the beef roast and vegetables I had put in the Crock-Pot this morning suddenly hit my nose like an iron fist. My stomach immediately started growling.

I still had some time before the roast was done, so I walked a few laps around the inside of the wall. The mental image I had of myself wearing that western gunbelt with sneakers, gym shorts, and t-shirt on a jog looked pretty ridiculous. And I wasn't yet familiar enough with the auto pistols to be comfortable carrying one of those instead. That was the reason for walking inside. And there was plenty of room to do it.

Someone had purchased several adjoining lots on this block to build on. The house and large garage-slash-storage building were halfway back, slightly left of center. The lots that this particular property consisted of stretched back to the next street over. By my estimation, the wall enclosed six square lots, two deep by three wide. And in this part of town, they were large lots to begin with. The gates and driveway were in the center of the front wall. The double gate was the only way in or out. The wall ran uninterrupted otherwise. There wasn't even a "people gate" anywhere. I had seen a few other places that had walls instead of wrought iron fences, but they all had a people gate. I don't know if the wall surrounding Victoria had a design flaw, or if the owners simply wanted as few openings as possible.

By the time I finished my fourth lap, I'd had enough. Each lot in this section of town was about sixty by eighty feet. And this place was three lots wide, two lots deep. Minus fourteen inches on all sides for wall width.

The door on the side of the house where I always sat outside led directly to the kitchen. So on my way to take a shower, I turned off the Crock-Pot. I didn't really care of the roast was done or not; I was going to eat anyway.

For some reason, food tastes better after a shower. Granted, it's kind of hard to mess up a meat slow-cooked all day, one of those "set it and forget it" kind of things. I guess the challenge will be if I ever try to fix something from scratch, something that takes more than one or two ingredients. If a Crock-Pot meal can get messed up, I'll be the one to do it. But I was hungry, and it tasted good. Besides, a little seasoned salt here and a little garlic powder there could probably rescue a lot of foods from entering the realm of doom. Or the disposal, whichever you want to call it.

Supper, tea, and a movie, my usual evening routine. Afterward outside with my CW and smoking. Again, the usual. It's getting a little monotonous around here. I'm going to have to shake things up a little. Tomorrow I might sit in the recliner while I eat.

# Chapter 15

I went back to the sheriff's office to make sure all the doors were still propped open. I emptied the gun cage and got all the equipment I might decide to use for something or other. I also decided that I would start driving one of the K-9 unit SUVs. I wanted to always have my rifle with me, and I didn't want to keep laying it on the floor of my Bus. After about an hour of messing with switches, dials, and buttons, I had the system fairly-well figured out. It would take a while to remember which button, switch, or dial did what, but I was confident I could do it. I had done a ride-along in a police car and an ambulance before, doing research for a book. I had forgotten anything I may have learned about their respective systems over the last few years. It was a refresher course at the very least. Speaking of ambulances...

I drove to one of the EMT shops, as I call them, and relieved one of the ambulances of its medical supplies. 'Cause you just never know.

Back to the Superstore. While some of the movies I had were worth watching a few times over, I wanted more variety. I got a flatcart and several large plastic totes. I tossed all of the movies from the cheap bins into them. The ones on the shelves, those formerly known as the more expensive ones, were easier to pick through and choose the ones I wanted to keep. But I wound up sweeping the lot of them into another tote. I'd go through them later. And I needed some more laundry soap. And dryer sheets.

I stopped at an electronics store on the way back to Victoria. My musical interests included classical, blues, jazz, bluegrass, REAL country music (not this new stuff wrongly called country), easy listening, hard rock, and heavy metal. Pretty much runs the gamut. I also discovered what they call "dark country." I really like it. The CD player at the house had a five-disc turntable, but I guess out of laziness I wanted something I could put a bunch of discs in and just let it go for a while. The choice was fairly easy. There were two models of jukebox-type CD players, a fifty-disc and a hundred-disc. I just grabbed one of each.

At the house, first thing was go through the CDs; keep what I wanted, toss what I didn't. Well, I didn't actually toss them, I set them aside with the movies I didn't want. Those would all go back to the store. I loaded up the smaller of the two players with a wide range of music. If the Rotts and cats had been capable of reasoning and rational thought, they probably would have thought I was a bit off.

# The Roanoke Effect

And I told them as much. George and Gracie were good listeners, but didn't have much to say. Chauncey and O'Malley didn't even listen. They were busy being cats, and that's a full-time job. While I put several styles of music in the player, I added more blues than anything else.

Music playing, drink on the coffee table, cigarette burning in the ashtray, I settled down to the all-important task of sorting through DVDs, Blu-Rays, and the rest of the CDs. Unwanted discs went into a tote all to themselves. And then a second one. Then there's a "Maybe" tote. There were quite a number going back, but not as many as I kept. After spending a few hours picking and choosing, then sorting by genre, I decided on a "Predator" marathon. Seven movies in quick succession. The prequel was great. Too bad there won't be any more. Breakfast and lunch had been a while back. The roast and veggies were gone at lunch, so canned stew was on the menu tonight. After supper and the first movie in the recliner (I told you I was going to shake things up), I migrated back to the couch. George and Gracie seemed to really like being beside me while I sat there. Truth be told, it felt good having them right there with me. After a quick bathroom break, I settled into the couch with my four furry folks to watch the second movie of the marathon.

I had gotten into the habit of doing what Emily called my "running commentary" during a movie or TV show. It was really nothing more than my guess as to whodunit, what was going to happen next, or maybe some historical fact behind a certain scene. Or even the historical accuracy, or maybe the lack thereof, of an entire movie. At some point during the second marathon movie, I dropped my guard. I turned to make a comment to Emily, only Emily wasn't there to comment to.

    I lost it.

    I leaned over and buried my face in Gracie's neck. I bawled my eyes out for I don't know how long. After a long bout of gut-wrenching, body-racking, heart-rending wailing, I got up and made a full pitcher of my CW, extra strong. Nobody was there to tell me that alcohol wasn't the answer. Even if they had been, I wouldn't have listened anyway. It was my answer right now.

    No more movies tonight. I went outside with the full pitcher, a glass, a bucket of ice, and a fresh pack of strawberry flavored little cigars. It was well past dark when I went outside. I wanted the dark, so I left the porch light off. I couldn't do anything about the street lamps. Actually, that wasn't strictly true. I could have shot them out, I suppose, but then I wouldn't know how to fix them when I decided that I wanted them back on after all. But it was still plenty dark on the porch, so I let that suffice.

# Chapter 16

I woke up on the couch, still fully dressed. How I got there: under my own power was obvious. When I got there: I had no idea whatsoever. I saw the Rotts staring at me.

"Why didn't you stop me?" I asked. George barked once. "You don't have to shout," I muttered. "Use your inside voice."

My rifle was standing up in the corner made by the couch and the wall. Gunbelt was on the floor. I sat up and waited for the room to stop spinning. When it finally settled down, I partook of the hair of the dog. And while I did, I checked the floor, furniture, walls, windows, and ceiling for bullet holes.

None.

Good. I hadn't gotten crazy last night. Well, not too crazy.

After I quit feeling as much like death warmed over, I made another trip to the Superstore in the cargo van. This trip was for some of those veneered pressboard CD and DVD shelves. It got old pretty quick digging through the totes, trying to decide which movie, or movies, I wanted to watch. After recent events, it was going to be a while before I watched another one. Unless maybe I happened to come across one that I knew Emily would absolutely loathe, despise, hate, and detest to the point that she wouldn't even consider watching it. But it would still be a while, even at that.

I made what I thought was going to be a quick detour by the books. I spent more time there than I thought I would. As a writer, or at least a former writer now, a book about libraries of the world caught my attention. There was a large section of coffee table books like that. I grabbed that one, and others about trains, bridges, lighthouses, sculpture, and courthouses. One about the famous Route 66 topped the pile.

Great. Now I was going to have to make a book run to the library. Which was fine. I really do like to read. Liking to read is a little easier on being a writer. It was just a lot easier to pop a movie in and veg out for however long I wanted to. Reading takes effort. More than I wanted to expend. Oh, well. It's time I gave my brain a little exercise, I guess. But I'll start off slow and easy. With one of the coffee table books. Then maybe I'll graduate to books about dogs running, and kids going down slides. But since my reading likes cross about as many genres as my music and movies do, I know I'll have a very large collection when I'm done.

A can of stew before I got started building those shelving units for the living room. A couple of hours later I was finished with all the shelves I had brought home.

Home.

I said the word several times. Each time sounded more and more hollow than the one before. Victoria wasn't home, it was simply a place to reside and exist right now.

I had been really hungry after putting all the shelves together, but not so much now. I forced myself to eat a can of clam chowder before grabbing my pitcher and pack of smokes. I had been doing okay up to that point.

Will it ever end?

## Chapter 17

Fall has fell, as they say, here in the mountains. It hits here sooner than most other places. At least that's how it seems. It was like flipping a switch: one night I was out on the porch comfortable in jeans and a t-shirt, and the next I had to come in early because it got too chilly for what I was wearing. Next trip to a store will include fall clothing. I may as well get some winter stiff while I'm at it.

The night before, I was unable to sit outside for as long, dressed like I was. So the next night I went into the study and slid a wingback chair over by the fireplace. Didn't really need a fire, but I lit one anyway. George and Gracie joined me, of course, but Chauncey and O'Malley stayed at their posts on the couch. Like concrete lions at the head of a driveway.

## The Roanoke Effect

I sat there long enough to go through the book documenting all of the lighthouses in the US, east, west, and south coasts; just like Florida's east, west, and south coasts. I finished my pitcher of CW and polished off a whole pack of the little cigars. I don't normally smoke that much. Usually a little more than half a pack in a day. While that would be very little for most smokers, it was a lot for me. Even back before I quit that was about all I did. On average. But on occasion, like that night, I went through a whole pack.

Long after the book was done, I sat smoking, drinking, and staring into the fire. No music, no movie, just the crackle of the fire accompanied by the occasional shifting of the logs. Smokes and CW were in easy reach. I got up for only two reasons: one, the bathroom, and two, to put more wood on the fire. I was definitely going to need to bring more wood in soon. And that was if I even went to bed. I did wind up sleeping, but in the chair, not the bed. After waking up with a stiff neck, I decided to replace the wingback with a foldout couch. All I had to do was bring one from the furniture store. None of the couches or loveseats at Victoria were sleepers. I could have moved the overstuffed recliner into the study, but the Rotts wouldn't fit up there with me. About the only place they didn't go with me was into the bathroom. But they did sit right outside the door and wait for me.

Because I didn't have a lot of experience chopping, cutting, and splitting firewood, I went driving around town looking for it. The grocery and convenience stores had some stacked up outside along the storefront year 'round. Two stops at convenience stores filled the bed of the pickup. After I unloaded back at Victoria, and then rested, I traded the pickup for the moving truck.

I have a confession to make: I'm not Superman. I thought I was in decent shape, but loading and unloading all that wood convinced me otherwise. And I had barely gotten started, as it turned out. A big hat-tip to all those who chop or cut, split, and stack firewood. Especially those who do it for a living. I hadn't done any of that yet, and I already didn't want to. But with all I picked up at the stores in town, it looked like I wasn't going to need to have to worry about it for a while yet. I wasn't exactly heartbroken over it. But I decided that I needed exercise, more than the once-occasional now non-existent walk with the Rotts. The walks were okay, but I obviously needed more. The pair of leather work gloves I got from the Superstore wore out in short order. Apparently they were only meant for light work. I had to go to the farm and ranch supply store for some good ones. And they have held up very well. It took a couple of days to get all the wood that I did. Even if there hadn't been as much as there was, any more would have to wait. I was sore in places I didn't know I had.

After a couple of days of recuperating, I was finally able to move around without whimpering too much. A two-wheeled wheelbarrow is much easier for getting more firewood into the house. And I didn't care one bit any mess I made with bark leaves, and dirt. I was more concerned about me than the floor. Besides, it was amusing to watch Chauncey and O'Malley, usually very dignified, batting chunks of bark around the kitchen floor. So when I cleaned up, I left several of the bigger pieces for them.

# The Roanoke Effect

My next trip to the Superstore was for some bottles of calcium and magnesium for the soreness. I had read that magnesium was good for muscles. And everyone has learned from milk commercials that calcium is good for the bones. After reading some labels I discovered that magnesium is the active ingredient in Doane's back pills. I also loaded up a couple of workout stations. Being that I had no spotter, the only free weights I used were the dumbbells and curling bar. But the two machines had pretty much any exercise I might want or need. After hand-trucking everything to the cargo van, my body confirmed my suspicion: I was not ready for any more exercise right now. When it got too cold to walk outside, I would come get a treadmill or something. But for now, a hot soaking bath, an actual meal (as opposed to canned stew), and then some relaxation in front of the fireplace. The sleeper sofa was a queen; plenty of room for the Rotts to join me. The cats must have felt left out. A few nights later they migrated to the office-slash-library and claimed their spots on the arms of the new couch. Every now and then they would go to the woodpile and sharpen their claws on the bark, then lie down in front of the fire for a bit before moving back to the couch.

My daily routine for about a week as I recovered from my firewood escapade was normally limited to eat, read, smoke, drink, sleep. Wash, rinse, repeat. Even the exercise machines had to be put together in stages. As well as moving the furniture to another room to open up floor space for the equipment. My physical condition was definitely not as good as I thought.

## David Nelson

      I was finally recovered enough to start exercising. Slowly. I learned my lesson. A few days of that and I was feeling even better. Plus it was time for that treadmill. So back to the Superstore I went. Since I couldn't decide specifically on what I wanted, I grabbed a treadmill, an elliptical, and a stationary bike. Why not? It's not like there was anyone around to give me a hard time about it. So I put them together in the living room, effectively turning it into my home gym.

      I had also decided to grab another flatscreen and Blu-ray player to put in the office, which had now become my living rom. While there wasn't a TV in the office when I moved to Victoria, there had been at one time. A cable box sat on a shelf, the coax still screwed into it. The cable to the TV was coiled up on top of the box. I connected the Blu-ray player to the TV and then, without thinking, I screwed in the cable box coax. When I did, a picture flashed on the screen for just a split second, then it was gone. I checked all the connections to make sure they were snugged up good. Then I froze. I had never even put a disc in the player. So what was that on the TV screen? Just a flash, then it was gone. It was a woman's face, and she looked really familiar. Probably from a show I had seen a long time ago. Or maybe someone from around town. But how could that possibly be? I'm the only human in town. Aren't I?

## Chapter 18

I had jumped back from the TV after the realization of no disc in the player hit me. Now the screen was blue, waiting for me to start a movie. I lit a cigarette and poured a drink. The ice rattled in the glass, I was trembling so bad. I stared at the blue screen, just waiting to see if it would happen again. I sat there for a good hour or so. Watching and waiting. Even George and Gracie were wary of the TV as they snuck past it. George barked at it a couple of times, hackles raised.

Nothing else happened in that hour, so I turned the TV off without watching anything. I spent the next few hours staring into the fire, smoking and drinking, trying to remember why that woman's face looked so familiar. The heater kicked on, and it startled me so much that I dropped my cigarette, spilled my drink, and almost fell off the couch. I was shaking as much on the inside as on the outside. If this kept up, I wasn't going to be worth a spit. My night was spent in fitful sleep, no rest whatsoever. My nightmare kept repeating. I saw the flash of the woman's face, and I could almost make out a word. I woke with a start more than once. I put the revolver out of easy reach because I didn't want to accidentally shoot one of the animals.

All the next day I had two nagging feelings that I just couldn't shake. First was that I somehow knew the woman I saw on the TV screen last night; and second, that I was being watched. By whom, by what, or even from where, I couldn't say. I continued carrying the Henry and wearing the gunbelt, but no longer simply because I liked the feel of them. Maybe I was getting paranoid. All I know is that things took a major turn for me that night.

I can't stand diet sodas. I also cannot stand beets, canned black-eyed peas, or garbanzo beans. And I needed to practice my shooting. Therefore, I had a nearly inexhaustible supply of targets to practice on. I would also be making more rounds through town looking for homes with any kind of weapons and ammunition in them. Although I would practice shooting everything I had at the moment, I planned on using the Henry and Ruger the most. Those were the ones I was most comfortable with now. On a lark I had taken to working on my fast draw. The .44 was unloaded, of course. But now I got more serious about it, because I didn't know but that it might be needed some day. I had dropped it many times inside on the carpet, so that's where I continued to practice for a while longer.

# The Roanoke Effect

With the revolver, indoor practice was for speed, and outdoor practice was for marksmanship. I missed more than I hit at first. But it wasn't too long before I was hitting more than I missed. In addition to the rifle and six-shooter, I also began carrying with me one of the 12-gauge shotguns from the sheriff's office. I had quite a variety of shells for it, but decided to keep it loaded with double-ought buckshot. I also chose a folding knife with a pocket clip, as well as a large bowie to carry on my gunbelt.

I remembered that a few of the houses where I had liberated some pets had some stuffed mounts on the walls. Which meant that most likely there were weapons of some sort inside. But I couldn't remember specifically which houses they were. So I was going to have to use the city map and go street by street, block by block, house by house.

I started at the farthermost point from Victoria, and once again worked my way around the grids I drew on the map. I also carried a different colored spray paint this time around. I used a bright red to mark the houses I checked, whether there were any guns or not. I also X-ed them off on the street map. Working at that for about three hours a day, it took a good three and a half weeks to check all the houses in town. I even took a 911 address map from the sheriff's office in case I decided to check houses outside city limits. Along with checking houses and businesses, I went ahead and cleared out the police station like I had the sheriff's building a few months back. I found a surprising number of weapons in the judge's chambers in the county courthouse and city hall both. I had read about such things, but had never actually seen it. I also had been loading up gun racks and cabinets when I could. The gun safes were mostly too heavy for me to handle alone. So I only took the lightweight metal ones, along with the wooden racks and cabinets.

It was getting colder and colder here in the mountains. I grabbed yet another city map and different color spray paint. This time my quest was for books and records I might want. When the Nightmare first started, I really did not like the idea of taking other people's things from their homes. Businesses were more impersonal, so I wasn't feeling quite as bad about them. But this far in, it was pretty good guess that none of these good folks were ever coming back. I had to be pretty selective, not so much with the records as with the books. Even with its two and a half stories plus basement, there wasn't unlimited space at Victoria. But entertainment was secondary to security; that's why I saved the book and record run for pretty much last.

It suddenly dawned on me one day that I was in need of a wardrobe change, and I don't mean just seasonal stuff. My body was responding to the exercise and work I had been doing. I needed a smaller waist in my jeans, and a bigger chest in my shirts. I was trying on a new pair of jeans. One leg in and I stopped, balancing on the other foot. A thought had just come to mind: while none of the steel gun safes I had checked were open, they were all unlocked. Who goes off and leaves a full gun safe unlocked like that?

What is going on here?!

## Chapter 19

The basement at Victoria had become an armory. I started feeling and smelling snow in the air, and I knew I didn't have long to get some things done. I took a storage shed kit from the lumberyard and got it assembled in record time. At least it was in my estimation. I laid in a large supply of bagged dog and cat food in the shed. The garage is heated, so I stored the canned food there. Then I went and got another load of groceries for myself.

I surprised myself by how much I was able to get done in such a short amount of time. Nothing like a good snowstorm, or possibly a blizzard, as an incentive to make sure you work faster. Also, I had hauled several deep freezes, upright and chest both, back to Victoria. One upright and a couple of the smaller chest freezers went in the kitchen, and the rest went into the garage. The garage was a four-car, plus extra storage space. I was able to keep Emily's car, my Bus and Bug, and the four-wheel-drive sheriff's SUV in there with plenty of storage space left for the deep freezes. And various and sundry things that I didn't want to junk up the house with.

So after the snow began to fall, I didn't go much of anywhere. I really didn't need to, as I had everything I might need or want at Victoria. If for some reason I'd need to go anywhere, I did have that four-wheel-drive. But I was neither expecting nor planning to.

I spent the winter sorting, arranging, and categorizing all the guns, ammo, books, movies, and music I had brought in. I took my time with it since I didn't have much else to do or anywhere to go. I watched some movies, but did more reading. Mainly the classics of both. I watched every Hitchcock and William Castle movie I could find, along with all of Universal's monster movies, Sherlock Holmes, the "Thin Man" series, a whole lot of noir, and a bunch of westerns. Books included Dickens, Melville, Milton, James Joyce, Hemingway, Edgar Rice Burroughs, and Dante. Plus all those coffee table books mixed in here and there.

While I was reading I would play a mix of toe-tapping jazz and blues with foot-stomping hard rock and heavy metal. For the times I just wanted to sit and stare into the fireplace, I had smooth jazz and easy listening going. Emily called me her Renaissance man.

Emily...

# Chapter 20

Winter settled into its usual routine. Grey skies, snow, wind, a little sun. A continuous cycle. Seldom a day above thirty degrees for almost five months. Usually. That's not always the case, but it's about average.

Along toward the last week of December, I did what I had done with the last week of November: put away all the calendars so I couldn't tell specifically that I was spending Thanksgiving and Christmas without Emily. Of course, I knew I was, I just didn't know exactly when the days passed. I plunged myself into my work of cataloguing an extra amount during those times. I would check, recheck, double-check, and cross-check everything until my eyes felt ready to fall out of my head.

Although there was no longer any cell service for the phones, they still kept time and date. So when I finally looked and saw that it was a few days into the new year, I decided to light off some fireworks of my own. Actual fireworks are (were) legal in town on only two occasions: Fourth of July and New Year's. Since the Nightmare started sometime after that first holiday and well before the second, there weren't any in town. So I would have to pull triggers instead of light fuses. Just firing off into the air seemed kind of boring, so I built a line of twelve snowmen, side by side, spanning the width of the street. On top of the head of each I placed a can of diet soda, like William Tell's apple. I spent most of an afternoon shooting my targets. From time to time I would stop and rebuild a few of the heads. That was usually after I used a shotgun on them.

One of the houses here had been home to at least one serious hunter, maybe more. Could have been the whole family, for all I know. Or maybe they were just ready if a war broke out in town. There were quite a number of mounts throughout the house, but there were enough handguns, rifles, shotguns, archery equipment, and bladed weapons to outfit a small army. One particular handgun was a .45-70. I didn't know exactly what that meant, and I wondered why someone had put a rifle bullet in a revolver. Anyway, I decided to give it a try. I aimed at a snowman's Tab hat, squinted down the barrel, and pulled the trigger.

I lay there for several seconds wondering why I had even tried that. That one shot told me that the gun was going to wait until spring to fire again, after everything was melted and thawed. I surveyed the carnage of the Diet Soft Drink Massacre, and decided that I'd had enough fun for

## The Roanoke Effect

one day. I had absolutely no idea how much brass and plastic was laying in the snow. But they weren't going anywhere, so picking them up could wait 'til the next day. I had parked the SUV with the back hatch facing the snowmen, as I had several different guns out there. I pulled back into the driveway and hit the remote to shut the gates. I pulled into the garage with the intention of carrying my cargo straight into the house from the garage. The gate had shut all the way by the time I pulled into the rightmost stall of the garage, just as I was about to hit the "Down" button by the door, I heard something. It was faint, but I would've sworn it sounded like an engine revving, as if someone was stuck in the snow. I had already opened the back hatch, so I grabbed the first long gun my hand touched. To be honest, right at that moment, I couldn't have told you if it was ever reloaded or not. That was a practice I hadn't quite gotten into yet. But I knew the Henry was, as I always make sure of it. Well, except for when I cleaned it.

    I hurried toward the gate, slipping and sliding the whole way. How I managed to make it to the gate without falling is a mystery to me. I stood there for a long while, just listening. I didn't even breathe for fear of missing something. I heard it again, once, even fainter than before, and only briefly. Another twenty minutes passed with no more of the engine sounds. I had to find out what was going on before I lost my mind. It was only then that the dogs barking caught my attention. They were both at the living room window, looking past me. The one time I left them in the house while I was outside. They were looking off to the southeast. It was almost dark, so any investigating would have to wait until tomorrow.

## Chapter 21

After I showered and warmed up a bit, I put on my PJ bottoms and a Ghoultown t-shirt. I got a good fire going, then went and got my pitcher of CW. On one of my last supply runs, I grabbed a box of cigars and a couple of pipes, along with the usual "accessories." One pipe in particular I grabbed because it looked like the one that Sherlock Holmes would smoke. I tried packing the pipe as best I could, just like I'd seen on TV. I finally got it lit with a disposable lighter, but only after burning my thumb and forefinger. Next time would be with a match. After puffing several times, I had a bluish cloud of smoke around my head. It wasn't very long before George and Gracie began sneezing. But then the heater kicked on and dissipated the smoke.

# The Roanoke Effect

I also decided that it was a Scotch night, so I put the CW back in the fridge and grabbed a bottle of eighteen-year-old Macallan. I guess maybe I was feeling a little bit sophisticated with the Holmesian pipe. If I wasn't careful, I might find myself looking for a deerstalker cap and a houndstooth cape-coat. I sat there sipping on my Macallan-rocks and puffing on my pipe. Cherry-vanilla, by the way, in case you were wondering. I was thinking about all the strange goings-on over the last several months.

First was all the vicious dogs that I rescued that showed no real interest in attacking me. None of them. At all. Very strange, that. Then there was the double gate at Victoria standing wide open. Others were closed, but not this one. Then the day that George and Gracie were barking at the gate, I thought maybe it was cats that got their attention. But when I checked, there was not the slightest trace of any animal outside the wall. No other dogs, no cats, not even a squirrel. The police and sheriff department gun cages were standing wide open. And that woman whose face flashed ever-so-briefly on my TV screen. I know her. I know I do. I just can't think from where, though. And in addition to the gun cages being open, all the gun safes in people's homes were also unlocked. Who goes off and leaves all their weapons available for the taking? And the latest, the sound of a revving engine. I'm beginning to think maybe I'm not as alone as I thought.

During the winter months, after all the necessary prep work was done is when I went to work on cataloging all the guns and ammunition. After all that was done, I had only the typical daily stuff to do. So I got bored. Very bored. To the point of single-character role-playing. I found various uniforms and period clothing sets at stores around town. We even had a small film production company in town. And by small, I mean the owner was also the director, producer, main writer, main actor, and PR officer, with a production crew of four others. Alex was a decent guy, pretty good at what he did, and he used mostly locals in his films. I read in the paper now and then that he even got screened at a few festivals. His studio was a source for some of my clothing and props. I told you I got bored. You can only read so many books, watch so many movies, and shoot so many hundreds of rounds before having to do something else.

So I went through the various incarnations: police officer, doctor, firefighter, old west town marshal, War of Northern Aggression soldier. I even put on a couple of steampunk costumes. Now I know that animals can't actually reason and rationalize, but the Rotts and cats had to have been thinking that I had finally lost my mind. You probably would have too, if you had seen me swaggering around the house daring outlaws to draw against me. Or dressed as a swashbuckler, swinging a cutlass, chasing other pirates. Or maybe as a mad scientist who almost blew up the house; I didn't do that one again. Or the surgeon who almost loses a patient, but saves the day (and the patient) in the nick of time.

Don't judge. You would probably do the same thing. Once I even put on medieval garb and did a one-man production of "Hamlet." The animals just stared at me.

# Chapter 22

When spring had finally sprung, it was none too soon. Cabin fever is a thing, believe you me. And it is compounded infinitely many times, as my geometry teacher would say, by the fact that I'm alone. At least I thought I was. Then again, maybe some things are just my imagination, and I was reading too much into others. I don't know. If I think about it too much, my head starts hurting again.

So as a distraction, I went and got a plow truck to start clearing the new slush off the streets. Just for something to do. The monotony was actually calming to me. Up one street, down the next. Back and forth. Up and down. I couldn't really tell if the Rotts liked it or not. I finally had to call it a day because the steady drone of the diesel engine almost put me to sleep a few times. A short nap later I was back out there clearing more slush. I cleared the gutters as best I could so that more runoff could go into the city drain system. My biggest concern was clearing a path from Victoria to the places that I went to most. The Superstore and a couple of grocery and convenience stores all had a fairly clear path to them. The rest of town would just finish on its own. At least for the most part.

As soon as I drove back to Victoria, I saw more confirmation that this place was devolving. A pack of eight or ten dogs, some of which I recognized as my rescues, were chasing a large house cat. And the dogs weren't playing, either. The cat made it up a tree to safety. The dogs were barking and snarling, trying to get to it. I stopped and watched for a few minutes. They never even looked my way. Their attention was soon diverted by something I couldn't see. Whatever it was led the dog pack to the end of the block and around the corner. I heard their barking and baying long after they were out of sight. The sounds finally melted into the air.

George and Gracie had been strangely quiet this whole time. Growling a little and huffing a few times was all the noise they made. Otherwise the Rotts just sat with perked ears, watching. Maybe they just had extremely good discipline. Whatever the case, I'm glad that pack didn't come my way. I wasn't real thrilled with that prospect, even if I was inside a locked vehicle. My mind flashed back to "Cujo." These dogs weren't acting rabid, though, just wild now. I guess feral is the word for a pet that has gone wild.

# The Roanoke Effect

I traded the plow truck for the SUV and headed to the store for more diet targets. On the way back to Victoria, I was watching for animal life, as always. I slammed on the brakes so suddenly that George and Gracie slid off the seats and onto the floor. In the snow were what looked like two sets of dog tracks. But they were bigger than any dog tracks I had ever seen. It appeared that wolves were coming down from the mountains.

## Chapter 23

Back at Victoria, I loaded several boxes of .44 and 12-gauge ammo into the SUV. I was also going to start practicing more with the auto pistols as well. Then I remembered that there was a left-handed holster with another .44 Ruger. I had been wanting one ever since I found that first one here at the house. So now whenever I went out, I had the two revolvers, the Henry, and a shotgun. I was twice as armed as before. If the wildlife was encroaching, I was going to need another way to get back inside the wall if they decided to show up while I was out target practicing. I was also going to be doing that right out in the street from now on.

Sawhorses from the county barn would be used setting my targets on now that there were no more snowmen. I used to worry about the mess I was making when I was doing target practice before. Now I really didn't care. I would grab some push brooms and trash cans for cleaning up my messes in the streets now, but that's only because that was the only place I would be practicing from now on. Or maybe I would try to figure out one of the street sweepers. I'll cross that bridge when I get to it.

I decided to put a ten-foot stepladder against the outside of the wall by where I would be shooting. Folded and leaning against the wall with the feet planted in the grass. I tied a piece of rope to the top of the ladder and threw the other end over the wall. That way if I had to make a quick getaway, I could climb up, grab the rope and pull the ladder up with me. In theory it worked. In practice it worked. I just hoped that I'd never have to test it in a real emergency. But I tried to be prepared. On the inside of the wall I had an extension ladder sticking a couple of feet above the top of the wall. I set the ladders a few feet apart so as to not get tangled up in them and do a swan dive into the grass. I don't think I would much care for that ten-foot free-fall. I'm sure I would break something, possibly my neck.

I made several more supply runs to get more food, drink, smokes, clothes, and fuel. And case after case of diet targets. I borrowed a truck from the furniture store because it had a lift on the back. At a construction yard I found seventeen empty and clean fifty-five-gallon drums. I loaded all of them into the truck, strapped them against the walls, and went to the gas station. I made a stop at Auto Zone to get what I hoped would be enough additive to keep the gas good. While I was there, I grabbed more oil for the lawnmower, as well as some two-cycle oil for the weedeater, hedge trimmer, and pole saw. The blower was electric.

Fortunately I had a couple of bottles left over after putting the requisite amount of stabilizer in each drum. Pumping over nine hundred gallons of gasoline gets rather boring. Or it would have if I hadn't been constantly looking out for unwanted visitors. George and Gracie helped keep watch. I knew they would hear or see something long before I did. So even though I kept looking outside, I watched them more.

Back at Victoria it seemed to take almost as long to unload the barrels as it took to fill them. I had to lower them a few at a time to the ground with the lift. Well, maybe I didn't *have* to do just a few each time, but I didn't want to take a chance of putting too much strain on the hydraulics. Fifty-five-ish gallons of gasoline, plus the drum itself, is kinda heavy. Using an appliance dolly, I hefted each barrel to the lift, and then to its spot in the garage. After the last barrel was in place, I drove back to the furniture store and got the Tahoe. At the house, I stripped down to my altogether outside and left the gasoline-smelling clothes by the side door. It took a while, and lots of scrubbing, but I finally got most of the gas smell off of me and out of my nose. It felt good to be able to just sit and do nothing after that day. This was going to be a Scotch, pipe, and Sherlock movie night. After that I might even read a little Lovecraft. Then again, maybe I'll leave the Lovecraft until the daytime, what with all the experiences I've been having lately. Yes, I think that might be the better call right now. So Sherlock it was. Two movies later I decided to watch the fireplace for a while. I began to wonder what other animals might be heading into town, if they hadn't already. In addition to the wolves, there were bobcats, mountain lions, and bears to be wary of. And the usual rabbits, deer, and elk. Come to think of it, I had been seeing more eagles and hawks flying around lately. A very majestic looking bird, the bald eagle.

That night I dreamed about my parents again. I dreamed that we were separated by a chain-link fence covered with plastic of some kind. I could hear them, but I couldn't see them. And no matter how I tried, I couldn't find the end of the fence. Either direction. Couldn't even see the top; it seemed to stretch upward for miles.

"We love you, Blake," my mom was saying. "Come back to us."

The heartache and heartbreak in her voice were so gut-wrenching, and so real, that I cried in my sleep. I missed everybody so much. How much more of this can I take?

## Chapter 24

The remnants of my dream echoed in my head after I woke up the next morning. "Come back to us." Come back from what? Come back from where? What did that mean? Or did it even mean anything at all?

I pondered on that as I walked several laps around the inside of the wall. The dogs walked with me, of course, but there was also a squirrel that decided to join us. He (or she; I couldn't really tell) would scamper along the top of the wall, stopping occasionally to chatter at us. I know it was the same one because of one tufted ear and one not, and a scar that ran from just under its ear and curved under its left eye. From a fight, I'm guessing. I wasn't sure if I wanted to see what it was the squirrel had fought with. I didn't care if it was a boy or a girl, I decided to name it Rikki, after Kipling's cobra-killing mongoose. I usually talked to

# The Roanoke Effect

George and Gracie as I walked, so I began including Rikki in the conversations. And I'll be dipped if it didn't seem as if that squirrel didn't understand every word I was saying. I'll admit, it seemed kind of spooky at first, but then I just decided I was the strange one, not Rikki.

After the first few times that Rikki joined us, I watched one day as he/she kept on going past us when I finished my walk. Along the wall facing the street, a left at the corner, then about a quarter of the way toward the back to a large oak tree. And jumped into the branches and disappeared.

One particular day I decided to make another book run, but for something I hadn't considered before. I went to the nearest law office and grabbed several volumes off the shelf. I put them in the Tahoe and went back inside. I got a cart and stacked as many books on tax law on it as I could, and rolled it to the dumpster. It was more symbolic than anything, but it made me feel better. Two more trips and I had them all. I might come back with some charcoal lighter and a match. This new penchant for reading law books probably won't last long, but, oh well.

I started reading one of them that night. And I understood very little of it. Lots of legal terms I had no idea what meant. Actus reus, mens rea, estoppel, demurrage, and moiety, to name but a few. I had briefly toyed with the idea of being a lawyer when I was in high school, but I'm glad that I decided not to. Too many tongue-twister words in the legal profession. But a few books I did force myself to read and study were first aid, EMT, and paramedic training.

Because I figured I might need to treat myself in case I got injured. You know, since there was nobody else here.

    I had no more oranges, and I couldn't find any learn-to-suture-at-home kits. I had read somewhere that porkbelly was good practice, but I wasn't sure if I had any of that either. I guess my practice will have to be on myself, should the time ever come. This was useful information. The law books weren't, really, so they went back the next week. I also decided to take a bottle of charcoal lighter and some matches for the dumpster. I squirted almost all of the fluid onto the tax law books. I doused the end of a stick with it, too. I lit the stick and stood well back as I tossed the temporary torch into the dumpster. A big *WHOOSH!* and away it went. I took the other law books back inside. The dogs went with me up to the third-floor library. I put them back on the shelf, then stood at the window and watched the fire burn from there. I lit a cigarette and smoked as I watched the flames below, and just flicked the ash onto the floor. It wasn't like I was going to get into trouble or anything. I crushed it out on the windowsill. I checked the loads in my .44s again. I unloaded one and practiced my draw some more. I kept the other one loaded. I practiced with my right hand for about twenty minutes before taking a break. I switched the unloaded gun to the left holster and lit another cigarette.

    The fire downstairs was burning low. As I watched it, I caught some movement out of the corner of my eye. A deer was standing in some high grass across the street, down on the next block. I think the movement I saw was its head coming up. It looked around before going back to browsing. But then I saw what the deer hadn't: a mountain lion creeping up behind it. I watched for what seemed like an hour. I thought about making some noise to scare the deer, but we all have to eat. The cat's patience and stealth were fascinating to me. I stepped back from the window to light a third cigarette, but when I looked back out, both deer and cat were gone. I decided that I didn't want to continue practicing. I reloaded the empty .44 and got ready to leave. I wanted to be away from there before it got dark. Meeting up with a cougar, day or night, wasn't something I wanted to do, but especially at night.

Because night comes earlier in the mountains, I didn't have much time. The sun was getting ready to dip behind the peaks, so I needed to move fast. Downstairs at the front door, I looked around very carefully to make sure the Rotts and I were alone. I saw nothing, which I knew didn't necessarily mean anything. I ran to the dumpster and closed the lids so nothing would float out and possibly set something else on fire. The dogs and I ran to the Tahoe. We all jumped in, I fired it up, and we took off.

For the next week I just hung around Victoria, doing target practice out in the street. Shoot, sweep, pick up. Shoot, sweep, pick up. I saw a bunch of rabbits, a few deer, but no more large cats.

I had gotten quite a bit better at hitting my targets, to the point of on occasion hitting the same can before it hit the ground. The glass bottles I had tried to reserve for the parking lot where I didn't drive, but I started using them in the street here. I just made sure to sweep a bit extra each time, and from time to time I would stretch the hose out to the street and give it a good spray. I wanted to try and get all the little shards of glass that I could. I really didn't want an animal getting a piece stuck in its paw. So I used very few of the glass bottles. Almost none. Just a few, but I may not use any more with the new wildlife population. And I had a seemingly endless supply of cans and plastic bottles anyway, plus all the canned veggies, salmon, and mackerel. I really had to clean up after the last two. Several cases of baking soda came in handy, let me tell you.

## Chapter 25

I seemed to have missed out on my chance to ride around town on a motorcycle. I just never got around to it, and there was no way I was going to now, not with that big cat in town. And wolves. And only the good Lord Himself knew what else came down from the mountains. I, too, wanted to know, but I didn't want to meet it. Whatever "it" was.

I was setting up some more cans on the sawhorses when I heard it. It didn't register at first, as I was keeping one eye on my surroundings and the other on my ladder. I had just cocked one of the Rugers when it broke through into my conscious: a chainsaw was being used by someone, somewhere. Or a small dirt bike. Either way, I now knew that I wasn't alone. I had to find out who else was in town with me. Was it a man? A woman? How many? How long had they been here? Where had they been staying? I had gone through every house and apartment in town. More than once. Whoever it was had hidden very, very well. My next question: how had they survived all this time? Either there was a bunker somewhere that I had missed, or maybe this person had been somewhere outside of town. That seemed more likely. I hadn't ventured past the city limits. Maybe it was time I did. Then again, if this mystery person was living outside of town, then why was he or she cutting wood in town? If he or she was indeed cutting wood. Again, it could have been a dirt bike, but I didn't think so.

    I had no idea how I was going to find this person. Or people. They're apparently very good at hiding. Except for that split-second blip on the TV screen, I'm the only person I've seen since the Nightmare began. Great. Another mystery to solve. I hadn't even solved the first one of where everyone went. Maybe I never will.

    I decided that the person or people weren't going to be found by my not doing anything. I made sure that all the .44s were loaded, Rugers and Henry, and then grabbed several others. An AR-10, a Glock .40, and my 12-gauge all went into the Tahoe, along with lots of ammo for each. Because you just never know. And now I couldn't decide if I wanted to take George and Gracie with me. On the one hand, I felt safer with them around. On the other hand, I didn't want anything happening to either one of them. I just couldn't bear the thought of losing one of them. Especially with all the wildlife in town. Plus, I had no idea if whoever might be out there was armed or not.

## The Roanoke Effect

I took them with me. If nothing else, I could always leave them in the Tahoe when I got out. I drove slowly toward the center of town. I saw several deer on the way, all grazing on the lawns. But I would no sooner see them than their tail would flip up and they'd be gone. At one point I saw a long tail disappear into a hedge. Same cougar or not, I had no way of knowing. Hopefully there was just the one in town, but that was highly unlikely. If there was one, there were probably several. It was foolish to think that there was only one around. And it was just downright dumb to even consider the possibility that there were no other dangerous animals in town. I had already seen wolf tracks.

I did see several pack of wild dogs. Some were chasing other animals, some were facing off with other packs. Animal turf wars, I guess. I wanted to honk the horn and run them off, but I just didn't want to alert the Unknowns to my presence any sooner than I had to. I wasn't one to set up an ambush, and I certainly didn't want to be the one ambushed. I watched and listened to the Rotts as much as I watched my surroundings. All the windows were open a couple of inches, for a couple of reasons. One, so the Rotts cold hear and smell better. Two, their breath was pretty bad, so I needed the fresh air. They were getting Milk-Bones when we got back to the house.

I drove slowly through different parts of town. I saw no one, just more animals. But I also saw lawns, shrubs, and flower gardens growing out of control. Some of the houses and sidewalks were in worse condition that I would have thought. It was almost as if time had sped up in random parts of town. Really weird. Other places looked as if they had been mowed, trimmed, and edged yesterday. And that was even weirder.

As I drove around, my stomach began to growl. And I hadn't brought anything to eat. I marked on the map where I had been. I had just put the map away and started off again when I saw something else move. I looked to my left and slammed on the brakes. I watched as a bear pushed over a chain-link fence as it left a back yard. George and Gracie went crazy inside the Tahoe. They wanted out. Whether to attack the bear or run away, I'm not sure. All I knew was that I wanted no part of it. I wanted to get out of there, but I couldn't move; I couldn't move my foot off the brake pedal. The bear then heaved itself upright and let out a roar that made my blood run cold. It had to be in response to the Rotts. If that roar was meant to scare the dogs, it didn't work. All it did was drive them into even more of a frenzy. But it sure scared the crap out of me.

How the glass in the windows didn't break with the Rotts going crazy like that is beyond me. It was only when the bear dropped back down on all fours and began lumbering in our direction was I able to do anything. I floored the gas, leaving dual tire marks on the pavement, and a ton of smoke in the air. And that's when the stupid hit. As I was driving forward, I was looking backward. My eyes were on the rearview mirror instead of the street. Because I was fixated on watching the bear chasing after the Tahoe, I didn't see the bull elk until after I hit it. Where it came from, I had no idea. But there it was. And I had no chance to step on the brake. I really had no idea how fast I was going since I never looked away from the mirror. As much damage as the Tahoe sustained, I had to have been going pretty fast. I was just glad that elk hadn't flipped up onto the hood. I'd read too many accounts of that happening, and those in the front seats getting kicked to death. It was probably because I never hit the brakes, and so didn't dip the front end.

Airbags deployed and the dogs yelped as they were thrown to the floor. It seemed much longer than it actually was for the airbags to deflate. I saw the elk scramble to its feet, then saw the bear fill the rearview mirror. It reared up again as it slammed into the back of the Tahoe, shattering the rear window. It tried to climb through the opening, but it was far too big. It roared as it swiped at George and Gracie. They were snarling and gnashing their teeth at the big beast, but were also keeping well away from its deadly claws.

I could smell the antifreeze on the ground, but an empty radiator and possibly burning up an engine were of no concern to me at the moment. After a few tries, the Tahoe revved back to life. I dropped the shifter into Drive and floored it once again. The bear hung on for only a short time before dropping to the pavement. My swerving from side to side may have something to do with it. Last I saw, the bear got up and chased after the elk I had just hit.

I drove like a madman back toward Victoria, hoping to get back before the Tahoe died on me. When it did, I was still an uncomfortable distance from the house. I let the truck coast as far as it would go before stopping on its own. I slammed my palms against the steering wheel several times as I yelled at the dead SUV before getting out. I kept looking around as I went to work. I pulled the driver's seatbelt out as far would go and cut it off at both ends. As best I could, I split the belt in two, down its entire length. Each narrow strip became a makeshift sling, one for the Henry, the other for the shotgun. The AR-10 I carried at the ready. I was really hoping that I wouldn't be needing more ammo than what was already loaded into the guns, because I had no way of carrying any more. I wasn't about to leave any of the guns in the Tahoe in case the Unknown found it. The ammo I would have to chance on still being there when I got back with the pickup. And then I was going to have to get another Tahoe.

George and Gracie stayed right with me as we headed toward Victoria. We had gone three blocks before I realized I had forgotten the gate remote. I cursed myself for my forgetfulness and jogged back to the dead SUV. After looking for longer than I would have liked, I finally found it under the front passenger seat. The impact with the elk had knocked it loose from its holder. Just as I turned around I heard the Rotts barking and snarling, and then what sounded like a woman's scream.

I froze. Not thirty feet away from me was a cougar. And not the one I had seen from the law office window. At least I didn't think it was. This one looked a little smaller. But then it looked gigantic. It ran a few steps toward me before launching into the air. It was already airborne before I had sense enough to raise the AR and shoot. I actually started shooting as I raised the rifle. Bullets ricocheted off the street, others plowed into the lawn, and still more hit the house just as fast as I could squeeze the trigger. I fired until the magazine was empty. And unfortunately only a few of the shots hit the big cat, none of them fatal. All I succeeded in doing was making it mad. When the cougar landed on me, I felt like I got hit by a truck. I was holding the AR out in front of me, by the buttstock and barrel. The cat's powerful jaws clamped down on the receiver. Because it was still cold here in the mountains, I was wearing a heavy coat. And it may have saved my life. That, and the fact that George and Gracie attacked the cougar to protect me. My coat was shredded, my body was bleeding, my adrenaline was pumping.

The Rotts succeeded in distracting the cat. It whirled and lunged first at one dog, then the other. They were quick and agile enough to keep away for the most part. If it had been only one or the other Rott, the cougar no doubt would have won. But because it was both of them, they were holding their own. I had sense enough to realize that I probably couldn't get the Henry unslung fast enough, so I reached for the Glock in my shoulder rig. I did not want to fire while the dogs were so close to the big cat. I waited a few seconds, leaning against the Tahoe, trying to steady my aim. Finally I yelled at the top of my lungs.

"HEY!"

The dogs skittered away from the cougar. It in turn spun around and looked at me, its tail flicking back and forth. The cat's eyes narrowed as it went into another crouch, preparing for another leap.

"LEAVE MY DOGS ALONE!" I screamed. I immediately fired, emptying the magazine. But this time almost every one of the fifteen rounds found their mark. The cat had just started to jump but only went a couple of steps this time before thudding onto the hard asphalt. I could feel myself leaning farther and farther to one side, and could hear the dogs barking again. Just before everything went black, I felt like I was moving. I remember thinking, "Great, it's dragging me off to its den."

# Chapter 26

I swam up through the inky blackness, trying to regain consciousness. I finally opened my eyes, expecting to see the Rotts, trees, pavement, and a broken-down Tahoe. I did see the dogs, but instead of the rest, I saw walls, a blond-haired woman, and the ceiling.

Wait, WHAT?! A blond? A woman? *Another human being?*

I tried to sit up, but firm yet soft hands pushed my shoulders down.

"No, lie back," a voice said. "You've lost a lot of blood, and almost your life."

The room began to spin when I tried to sit up. The spinning in turn made my stomach flip. I rolled onto my side and got sick. My new benefactor was apparently expecting that because she was tight there with a wastebasket. After my stomach finished heaving, I lay back trying to catch my breath. I had forgotten how much throwing up took out of a person. No pun intended. I had also forgotten how unpleasant it was. I wished I hadn't been reminded.

After the room settled back to not spinning, I looked around. I did recognize my surroundings. I was back at Victoria, in my bedroom. The one I hadn't slept in for some months now. I started to scratch my chest, but there was a large bandage wrapped around my torso, from pits to waist. That's when I noticed the bandages on my arms as well. Then I raised the sheet. At least I was wearing a pair of gym shorts. That was a relief.

At the foot of the bed George and Gracie sat watching me. I turned my head slowly to the left. Slowly so as to not get sick again. There she was. The blond. I knew her from somewhere.

"Don't scratch," she said. "You're healing. I know you want to, but don't. Because then I'll have to clean and stitch you up again."

"You stitched me up?" I asked.

"Just the worst ones," she said. "The lesser ones I butterflied."

"Thanks." I continued to scan the room. I didn't see my clothes anywhere. I didn't see my guns anywhere either. And the Rotts weren't acting upset with her.

# The Roanoke Effect

"You're back at your house," she said.

"I know. I recognize my room."

We stared at each other for several long moments before I began looking around the room again. She got up and left the room. I heard her go downstairs, and in about half a minute I heard footsteps coming back upstairs. She came into the room carrying one of my gunbelts. She must have seen the concern on my face when she returned because she put the gun and holster on the bed beside me.

"You looked like you wanted one of these. And you can relax. If I, at best, didn't care about your wellbeing, or at worst, actually wanted you dead, I would have left you lying in the street."

As I mentioned, the dogs didn't seem upset at her being there, and I trusted them. But it was more than a little unnerving to be alone –completely and utterly alone– for all this time, and then someone just suddenly swoops in to save the day. I appreciated it, don't get me wrong. It was just really unsettling. But at least I didn't have to sew myself up. Not sure if I could have done it. I hadn't said anything to her since she came back; we just kind of watched each other for several minutes. Finally she stood again.

"I'll be back shortly," was all she said before leaving once again.

The Rotts watched her leave, then looked back at me. I patted the bed.

"Come on."

Right away they jumped up on the bed and laid down by my feet. I listened as the blond made her way downstairs. I checked the .44 to make sure it was still loaded. I clicked around each chamber, one by one, not spinning the cylinder like on TV. Good way to ruin the mechanisms, I had read.

It was still fully loaded.

I had just reholstered the Ruger when I heard her coming back up the stairs. She came into the room with a large mug in hand. Whatever was in it was hot, as there was steam rising from it.

"I brought you something," she said.

"I have two questions for you," I said in response.

"What?"

"First, what is that?"

"Beef broth."

"Second, who are you?"

"Fair question." She set the mug on the nightstand. "My name is Alexandra Moore. Allie for short."

"Where are you from?"

"That's three questions," Alexandra said.

I just looked at her. She smiled sheepishly.

"Too soon for a joke?"

"I'm not in much of a joking mood right now."

"Okay," she said. "I'm from here, actually."

"Where do you live?" I took a sip of the broth. It was good.

"A couple of miles north of town."

"Why haven't I seen you before?" I asked. "Why are you just now coming into town?"

She looked at her hands for several seconds before answering. "Because I was scared."

"Scared? Scared of what, Alexandra?" I sipped some more.

"Allie, please."

"Scared of what, Alexandra?" I asked again.

She let out a heavy sigh. "First of all, I was scared out of my wits at being left all alone. And then second, I was scared of all the gunfire I started hearing."

"Fair enough," I conceded. "But what about food and supplies?"

"I have a few acres with a large garden and some livestock. As for other supplies, I just made do with what I had, for the most part."

"Why did you come to town to cut firewood?"

"I didn't. I was at home cutting. Sound carries far on a cold day. And I had forgotten that at the time."

"So this is the first time you've come to town?" I set the now-empty mug back on the nightstand.

"No, this is just the first time you've seen me." She reached for the mug. "I came into town a few times at night to try and figure who it was shooting so much."

"You mean you've never come into town during the day?"

"Once before."

"How did you know where to bring me?"

"The dogs led me here."

I was getting tired of this question game.

"By the way," she said, "I've seen you before."

"Where?" I asked. "When?"

"Around town. Before all this happened."

"How long have you lived here?"

"All my life. As I said, I'm from here."

I was quiet for several minutes. Alexandra left with the mug, and me lost in thought. When she came back, she still had the mug, and it was steaming again. It was more broth.

"Is there anything you want or need?" Alexandra asked.

"Yes, as a matter of fact there is," I said.

"What's that?"

"I want to go downstairs to the library where my smokes, my couch, my fireplace, and my Scotch are."

"You probably shouldn't be doing much drinking right now."

"Really?" I asked. "And why is that, pray tell? Who died and made you Mom?" I snapped.

Alexandra looked genuinely hurt. Her eyes welled with tears. "I gave you some heavy-duty painkillers," she whispered. "They don't mix well with alcohol. That's all." She walked to the bedroom door and stopped. "I'll go now," she said without turning, "and leave you alone. The pain meds are in the top drawer of the nightstand." She let out a long, ragged sigh. "I didn't mean to intrude."

And with that Alexandra Moore walked out of my life as quickly and suddenly as she had walked into it. I heard her sniffing and ragged breathing as she made her way downstairs. The front door opened and closed. A vehicle started up. The gate opened. The vehicle faded a little as Alexandra backed out of the driveway. I heard footsteps headed back toward the house. I thought maybe Allie was coming back. Then I heard the gate start to close, and what sounded like her walking fast. Then she was gone.

Allie. I thought of her as Allie, not Alexandra. But it didn't matter now, one way or the other. She was gone. The one other person around, one who had shown me care and concern, was gone now because I was an ass. A grade-A, number-one, government inspected ASS. I know it was the pain talking, but it was still no excuse for the way I treated the one who had most likely saved my life. The dogs would barely look at me now. It was as if they actually understood what had just happened.

I tried to lean over and get the painkillers out of the drawer. The eruption of pain was so intense that I screamed and almost passed out. When I finally recovered, I tried again. The first time I reached across myself with my right hand. Purely out of habit. This time I felt around with my left hand. It was difficult trying to do it all by feel, fumbling around like that, but I managed. Looking at the bottle I saw that the pills were ten-milligram hydrocodones. The thing is, I didn't know for sure when Alexandra had given me the last pill. And I hadn't thought to ask, so I had to take my chances. After about an hour or so, I could feel it starting to kick in. I was still hurting, I just didn't care as much now. Soon I was asleep again.

I didn't know how long I slept since I didn't check the time. It was dark when I awoke, and it had been light when I fell asleep. I saw the urinal on the nightstand for the first time. I used it, not trusting myself to walk just yet. I fell back to sleep.

When I awoke the next time, I was hungry. And there wasn't any food in the room, just an hands empty mug and a partial bottle of water. How was I going to do this? My legs were fine. It was my arms and chest that had gotten mauled. Maybe if I slowly slid my legs toward the side of the bed, I could somehow work my elbow under me enough to push myself up to a sitting position. I was going to have to figure it out somehow. I got myself turned a little, enough to hook my leg down the side of the bed. That, combined with my elbow, got me to sitting up on the side of the bed. More waiting for the dizziness to subside. I stood up slowly, fumbled with the gunbelt and finally got it buckled on as best I could, grabbed the pill bottle, and eased my way toward the staircase. I didn't have to call the Rotts; they were beside me the whole time.

At the top of the stairs I couldn't decide if I wanted to try walking down, or sit down, and do it that way. I decided to try walking. Holding onto one railing with both hands, I descended one step at a time, pausing on each. The dizzy was coming back. Halfway down, I had to sit and finish that way. Then I had to stand up and walk to the kitchen. By the time I was able to fix myself something to eat, my arms were on fire.

The next week added a physical hell to the mental and emotional one I had already been in for the last almost year. I know I had to move my arms around some to keep them from getting too stiff, but I didn't move them much more than I had to. After the second week I was able to move a lot more freely. By the third week, I knew that my stitches would have to come out at some point. I could reach most of them, but some I couldn't. I had to leave those alone for the time being.

## Chapter 27

I kept telling myself that Alexandra didn't want to see me again. What I was actually doing was putting off trying to find her. I knew I needed to, even if just to apologize. I drank half a bottle of Jameson trying to numb my shame and embarrassment over how I had treated her the first day. I finally decided that I was sufficiently numb and artificially courageous enough to go looking for her place.

I remembered Alexandra saying that she lived a couple of miles north of town. The problem was that there are three roads leading out of town in a northerly direction. And it would be just my luck, and serve me right, if it was the third road I chose. And sure enough....

# The Roanoke Effect

The first highway out of town had no residences at all for at least five miles. I don't know about farther because that's where I turned around. Eventually. It took a few tries, but I finally got it done. The second highway was actually a farm road, and there were no signs of life at any of the houses out that way. Again, five miles, then I turned around. The third highway was where Alexandra lived, but she was three miles out of town, not a couple.

I was driving slow for two reasons. First because I didn't want to pass her house by accident. Second, I had downed half a bottle of Irish whiskey and didn't want to be going fast in case I ran off the road. I saw a tendril of smoke rising from behind a line of trees, and there was an overgrown lane that disappeared behind them. My response time was compromised, and I passed the driveway. Again, I had to turn around. So I did. Eventually.

The house was a couple of hundred yards off the highway, hidden by the trees. Completely out of sight from the road. The smoke I saw was rising from the chimney. I had barely come to a stop when Alexandra came out the front door. She wasn't curious about who it was (obviously), but she was angry that it was me. And understandably so. She also had a gun in her hand.

"What are you doing here?" she demanded as I almost fell out of the truck.

I closed the door and leaned against it. "I came to apologize for how I treated you."

She walked over to me. Studied my face for a few minutes in silence.

"I'm sorry," I said.

Alexandra leaned in a little and sniffed a couple of times. "You've been drinking." A statement, not a question.

'Yes," I said. "A lot."

"Why?"

"Because I couldn't stand face to face with you if I was sober, as ashamed and embarrassed as I was...am...about how I spoke to you."

She snorted in derision. "You're barely standing at all." She shook her head at me. "Go up on the porch and sit down before you fall down."

I took a couple of steps, then stopped. "Wait," I said.

"Go sit down," Alexandra repeated. "I'll get them."

I staggered toward the porch, almost tripping over a chicken, while Alexandra let George and Gracie out of the truck. I stumbled up the steps and fell into a chair. The Rotts barely even looked at the chickens pecking around the yard as they came up on the porch with me. Alexandra went inside and came back out with a steaming cup. She held it out to me.

"Drink," she said.

"More broth?" I asked.

"Coffee. Drink."

"Yes, ma'am." I gave an exaggerated salute.

If looks could kill I would have been severely wounded, at the very least. I drank my coffee. Sipped it, actually, because it was plain black. I was still drinking it back at Victoria with sugar and powdered creamer or sometimes canned milk. But usually just the creamer. She went and got a cup for herself.

"What's the real reason you're here?" she asked. She sat down in a chair opposite me.

"To apologize, as I said, and to ask you two questions."

"What questions?"

"First, will you forgive me for being such an ass?"

She said nothing, just looked at me. Her expression did not bode well.

"What's your second question?" she asked.

"I was wondering if you would take my stitches out."

"That's a statement, not a question."

"Would you take my stitches out?"

Alexandra regarded me with a cool, almost cold, stare before she answered.

"Yes, to the second. I don't know, to the first. That's going to take some time."

"I'm sorry."

"I heard you the first time." She set her cup down. "Come inside so I can take a look at your wounds to see if they're ready."

I gulped the rest of my coffee. It scalded all the way down. But it woke me up. I followed her to the kitchen.

"Sit down," she said. "I'll be back."

When she returned, Alexandra was carrying what looked like a tackle box. It was her first aid kit. Rather than take the time to unwrap and unwind all the gauze, she used EMT shears to just cut i off a layer a time. She was very gentle as she pulled the bottom layer away. A few pieces required some warm water to release the bandage from a scab.

"You didn't do too bad of a job changing these yourself," she said. "Or cleaning the wounds." No praise or impress in her voice, just matter-of-fact.

"It wasn't easy."

"But you managed."

I didn't say anything else as she worked on me. Most of the stitches came out. Those in the deepest gashes she said to leave in for another week. Although she took it slow, and I'm pretty sure she wasn't trying to deliberately hurt me, my skin was burning where Alexandra pulled the sutures out. Several firm presses of a clean bandage later had the blood ooze cleaned up. Next she applied more triple-antibiotic ointment and covered them again. Just some individual bandages this time, not complete wraps.

"There," she said, "you're done. Now go sleep it off on the couch. Then you can go home."

"Thank you for doing that," I said. She just looked at me. "Why are you acting like this? I asked. "I said I was sorry."

"And I said I heard you."

"Look, I was way out of line..."

"Yeah, I'll say."

"...snapping at you like I did. I was in excruciating agony. I've apologized. Why are you treating me with such hatred?"

"I used to think you were a nice person."

"'Used to'?"

"A couple of weeks ago made me think differently."

"Why, because I snapped at you in my pain?"

Alexandra was silent for a moment. "You don't remember, do you?" she asked.

"Remember what?" I asked in return. "We just met recently, and the one time. What is there to remember?"

"I met you and your wife some years back at a book signing. I had every one of your books, and I couldn't wait for you to sign them. Everyone else had one book, your latest. I had a whole stack. You and your wife...what was her name?"

"Emily."

"Right. You and Emily took the time to talk to me, to listen to me, while you signed every book I had. Neither of you acted the least put out with my having more than one of your books to be signed. You listened as I told you what had happened the year before, and that your stories were a wonderful escape for me."

"You lost your husband and your son." I began to mentally kick myself.

"Yes. So you see, it wasn't that you snapped at me, or spoke harshly because of your pain. Everybody does that. It wasn't how you said it." A tear escaped and rolled down her cheek. "It was what you said."

That's how I knew her. That's where I remembered her from. I broke down.

"I'm sorry," I said. "I am so, so sorry." I buried my face in my hands.

I don't know how much time passed. It could have been a few minutes, it could have been an hour. I just don't know. But the next thing I knew, I felt her hands on mine.

"Hey," she whispered.

I couldn't look at her.

"Hey," she said again. "Look at me."

"I can't." Barely a whisper.

"Look at me." She put her fingers under my chin and brought my head up. "I believe you," she said softly. "I believe you."

I pulled her close and cried into her shirt. All the frustrations, anger, upsets, and sadness from Emily dying, the Nightmare beginning, and everything else up to this point just came pouring out. The dam had burst, and there was no stopping it. Again, I have no idea how much time passed. It seemed like hours. I was physically and emotionally spent.

I let go and leaned back. There was a box of Kleenex on the table. I wiped my eyes with one and blew my nose with another.

"I'm sorry," I said. "I got snot all over the front of your shirt."

"It's okay," she said. "It'll wash out."

"Allie, will you forgive me?"

She knelt in front of me and cupped my face in her hands. "Yes, Blake, I forgive you."

Blake. I hadn't heard anyone say my name since it all began. It actually sounded strange at first. And I called her Allie. On purpose.

## Chapter 28

We spent the next several months getting to know each other better. And she still had my books on her bookshelf. Her main interests were hunting and fishing, romance novels, easy-listening music, and chick flicks. We were about evenly split for a while. I would go see her out at her place, then she would come into town to Victoria. And that's how it stayed for a long time, maintaining our own residences. But I did give her her own gate remote, so there was that. And we had police radios to keep in touch. The only guns Allie had at her place were a .243 rifle and a .38 Special snubnose. I told her to come to the house and take what she wanted from the basement-turned-armory. She took two 12-gauge shotguns, one each .308 Winchester and 7mm Remington Mag rifles, and a .357 Colt Python. Plus a couple of cases of ammo for each.

# The Roanoke Effect

Whichever place we happened to be, we always took time to sit on the porch. Me with my usual smokes and various whiskeys, Allie sipping either iced tea or a glass of wine. Time seemed to fly by after that. I had someone to actually talk to again. Nothing against the Rotts or cats, but they weren't real big on conversation.

Allie had no actual pets, just her few chickens, so she and the dogs and cats just kind of adopted each other. We did a lot of target shooting together, drove around town a bit, watching it slowly being reclaimed by the wild. But mostly we would sit and talk. Just talk. It had been so long since either of us had had any human contact, we just liked to hear someone else's voice for a change.

"That time I came to town during the day," Allie said in one of our early conversations, "I went to the TV station to try and make a video. I wanted to broadcast it on a loop in case there was someone else out there."

"I was here."

"But I didn't know that at the time. And then I heard all the shooting, and got too scared to come back during the day."

"So what made you come back the day I got attacked?"

"I don't know. I guess I thought I needed to restock a few things I had run out of. I really don't remember now. But I'm glad I did. You might have died."

"Thanks to you, I didn't." We sat in silence for a bit. "And your video idea worked for only split second," I continued, "because I saw the barest flash of you on my TV screen."

"What are you talking about?" Allie asked.

"You just said you made a video to play on a loop in case someone else was out there."

"No, I said I tried to. I couldn't get the camera figured out. I never made the video."

# Chapter 29

As spring turned into summer, the power at Allie's house went out. It happened when a squirrel caused a transformer to blow. I was doing my laps inside the wall when the gate began to open. I knew who it obviously was. That's not what put me in defense mode. I was watching to make sure that *only* Allie came through the gate. Rabbits, deer, and elk would most likely shy away from vehicles and walls that suddenly made noise and started moving. I wasn't so sure about the predators out there; the bears, cats, and wolves. And wild dogs. I'd had an idea for a platform of some kind as a retreat rather than try and make it back inside, but just hadn't done anything about it yet. So as soon as I heard the gate, I held my rifle at the ready, waiting to see if Allie was bringing in any unwanted company. Fortunately, none had thus far made it inside, but there's always a first time for everything.

She pulled into the driveway and the gate began to its closing roll. Just as the two sides came together, something slammed into the outside of the gate. Hard. The gate was less than six inches from the top of the wall, and each half rolled on a wheel and was maybe four inches off the ground. I didn't have much fear of any predators climbing over, and I was pretty sure anything capable of that much noise wouldn't fit underneath.

All of a sudden something started pushing the gate inward. I heard animalistic grunting and heavy breathing. At the bottom of the gate were large hairy feet with giant claws. A bear was pushing against the gate.

"Get the crossbar!" I shouted as I ran toward the gate. Allie jumped out of her truck and ran back to get the crossbar laying by the wall. She dragged it toward the gate as I was trying to drop the steel rods into their slots in the concrete. The two horizontal slide bolts I had installed not long after I moved in might have to wait until the crossbar was in place. I managed to slip one of the steel rods into its slot, but was having a hard time with the other. The bear was preventing it from sliding home.

The crossbar was pretty heavy, so when Allie got it dragged over we both picked it up to put it in place. We set it on top of the brackets so that it would fall into place when the bear let go of the gate. The grunts turned to growls and then roars. The Rotts weren't really helping either with their barking. I kept hollering at them to stop, but they weren't listening. Not this time. The crossbar finally fell into the brackets. I got the other steel rod dropped into its slot as well. I got the bottom slide lock pushed into place and climbed up to engage the top one. As I climbed, the bear hit the gate again, knocking me from my perch. I landed flat on my back, the wind knocked out of me. I also hit my head on the concrete. It didn't knock me out, but I couldn't move, although I knew I needed to.

"Blake!" Allie screamed. Everything went all of a sudden into slow motion. Allie ran over to check on me, but I managed to point at the gate. She left my side, and then I saw her truck moving. I managed to roll over onto my side, then my stomach. Getting my hands and a knee under me, I was finally able to get up on all fours. I felt arms around me, trying to lift me.

"Let's go," Allie urged. "Stand up."

I made it to my feet and we stumbled toward the porch. After a few slips and false starts I made it up the steps. A few seconds later and we were inside. Allie helped me to the nearest chair.

"Wait here," she said. "I'll be right back."

Either I passed out or Allie moved really fast. Because it seemed like she hadn't even left after saying that. But I know she did because she had my rifle in her hands.

"I think we're safe now," she said. "I parked the truck against the gate and got the top slide lock engaged." She looked into my eyes, from one to the other, back and forth. "How are you feeling?"

"My head hurts."

"It's probably going to hurt more. I apologize in advance."

"What are you...aaaaagh!"

Allie gently pressed around on the back of my head for a few seconds. "The bump is forming. That's good."

"Why is that good?" I asked. "It hurts."

"Because if there's no bump, or knot, that would mean it was going in. And that would not be a good thing. Outside bump, good; inside bump, bad."

"Then I'm glad there's a knot."

"Let me get some ice for it." A few seconds later I heard the ice machine in the freezer spitting cubes into a plastic bowl.

"Could you drop a couple of those into a glass with some Dewar's for me?

"You want that, or do you want a painkiller?"

"I want the Scotch. And a cigarette."

Allie came back into the living room. "Would you take those to the library for me?" I asked, pointing to the drink and ice pack. "I want to go sit in there instead."

"Okay, hang on."

She came back in less than a minute to help me walk to the other room. I was unsteady and leaned heavily on her shoulders.

# The Roanoke Effect

"We have got to stop doing this," Allie said.

"Stop doing what?"

"You getting hurt and me coming to your rescue."

"Well," I said, "if the wildlife would just leave me alone, this wouldn't keep happening."

"I know," she said. "They are so inconsiderate."

"Tell me about it."

In the library we made our way to the wingback. I put the footrest up, set the ice pack between my head and the chair. I took a sip of Scotch. Allie asked me if I was set.

"For now," I said. "In a little bit I'll need to change into some shorts and a clean t-shirt. But that's later. Right now I want a short relax, a drink, and a smoke."

"Okay." Allie untied my bootlaces and dropped the heavy steel-toes on the floor with a thud. "Better?"

"Yes. Thank you."

"Is there anything else you need?"

"Yes, actually, there is."

"What's that?"

"I need to get these gunbelts off."

"Oh. Right. Here, let me help you up."

"I'm sorry," I said. "I should have thought of this before I sat down."

"Don't worry about it," Allie replied. "Actually, wait a minute. Let me go get your shorts and shirt. That way you can take care of all that at one time."

"Okay. That'll work."

Allie normally slept upstairs when she stayed here, since I had been living in the library for quite a while now. But I had a feeling that maybe she would want to sleep downstairs tonight. Also whenever she was here, one of the Rotts followed her around the house like they always did me. Gracie usually slept upstairs with Allie while George stayed with me. When Allie got back I took it slow getting to my feet to unbuckle my gunbelts.

"Do you think maybe you should take a shower before you get too comfortable?" she asked.

"Yeah, maybe I should," I said. "Once I get settled into the chair, I know I won't want to get up again."

"Okay. Just be careful."

"I'll try."

Fortunately the library had a three-quarter bath attached to it.

"Be warned," Allie said. "If I hear you fall, I'm coming in."

"Understood," I said. "I'll try not to."

It took a while, but I managed to shower without incident. I dried off, got dressed, and made my way back to the chair. Allie went and refreshed my ice pack. Then she went upstairs. When she came back down, she was wearing another of my shorts and shirts.

"I'm sleeping in here tonight," she said, "so don't even try to argue with me."

"Okay."

"Not a word. You've been injured and...wait, what?"

"I said 'okay'."

"Oh. Okay. Good."

I took another sip of my drink. Allie came and knelt beside the chair.

"Is there anything else you need right now?"

"Well, if you don't mind, my Holmes pipe, tobacco pouch, pipe tamper, Scotch bottle, and some more ice."

"Okay." She looked at my eyes again. "How's your head? How's your vision?"

"Head hurts. Vision okay."

"Ugh. Okay. You sound like caveman."

"Sorry."

"Lighten up, I'm just messing with you."

"Okay," I said. "Sorry."

"Quit being so sorry." Allie stood up. "Don't move. I'll go get your things." She leaned down and gave me a quick peck on the cheek.

## David Nelson

It surprised me. Nothing like that had happened until now. I turned and looked at her. She hadn't pulled back; our noses were almost touching. So I kissed her. And she kissed back.

# Chapter 30

I slept in the chair that night while Allie slept on the couch. She was going to sleep on it as it was, but I talked her into folding it out so the dogs could sleep up there too. The next morning I awoke to the smell of bacon, onions, and potatoes frying. I staggered to the bathroom, then staggered to the kitchen. Allie also had some eggs. Real, honest-to-goodness eggs. I hadn't had eggs in a very, very long time.

I managed to pour myself a cup of coffee and had half of it gone before I noticed the ice chest on the floor.

"Where did that come from?" I asked, pointing at it.

"I brought it in yesterday," Allie said. "The power went out, so I just put the cold stuff in a couple of coolers and brought them here."

Oh, okay." I finished my first cup. "How long have you had these eggs?"

"I gathered them yesterday morning. Then a transformer blew. I have no clue how to reset it. Or whatever is done to fix one." She began cracking eggs into the skillet. "And when the coast is clear, we'll go get the rest of my things." Allie looked at me. "Looks like you now have a roommate." She turned back to the eggs, but right away looked at me again. "If that's okay," she added quickly.

"That would be great," I said. "There's strength in numbers."

Allie didn't turn around this time. "Is that the only reason?"

I poured another cup. Smaller amounts of creamer and sugar. Trying to get used to just plain black. That way I wouldn't have to worry about anything, I can just pour a cup and go. "No," I said. "It's not."

"How do I know that?"

"Well, I distinctly remember kissing you last night. And believe me, I didn't do that lightly, or for no reason."

Allie transferred the fried eggs from the skillet to a paper towel-covered plate. Then she turned around and leaned against the counter.

"So what are we going to do?" she asked. "How is this going to work?"

"Well," I began, "I guess for now we'll keep doing what we've been doing: you upstairs in my old room, and me downstairs in the library."

"Really? So you can keep hogging the fireplace all to yourself?" Her voice was serious but her eyes were smiling.

"Okay then, I'll take the room upstairs and you can have the library."

"Or," Allie countered, "we could move another couch into the library, and that way we can share the fireplace."

I pursed my lips and stroked my chin as if in deep thought.

"How about this? We go to the furniture store and get another foldout couch to put in the library. That way we could share the fireplace while it still gets cold at night."

"That's a good idea," Allie said. "Glad I thought of it."

I walked over to her. "Seriously," I began. "Are you sure you want to stay here from now on?"

She stood up on tiptoes and kissed me lightly on the lips. "Yes, I'm sure."

"Okay. Then we'll bring your things back here. Then go get another couch for the library. I don't think we'll need the moving truck for that."

"Sounds like a plan," Allie said. "Now go sit down. Breakfast is ready."

We ate in silence. I finally pushed my plate away, and sat back. Allie poured me another cup of coffee while I lit a cigarette.

"Was the food okay?" she asked. "Did it taste alright?"

"Did you hear me talking?"

"No."

"Exactly."

"I'm glad you enjoyed it."

"One question though."

"What's that?"

"Why have you never shared your eggs before?"

"Because, quite frankly, I was selfish." She let out a heavy sigh. "I had a limited supply, and I didn't want to share them. And then it occurred to me how much of a witchy woman I was being. So I started saving them for the last week and a half or so, and now they're in the fridge."

"So what are your plans for the chickens?" I asked. "You won't be out there to take care of them, so what's going to happen to them?"

## The Roanoke Effect

"Well, that's something I wanted to talk to you about."

"Okay, I'm listening." I grabbed my coffee and cigarettes. "But let's go in the library. It's more comfortable in there."

Allie spent the next half hour telling me about a place south of town that was similar to Victoria, only bigger.

"It sounds like a great place," I said. "But moving all this stuff again? I'd rather not."

"But you'd have help this time."

"This place has kind of grown on me now."

"Fungus grows on you too, but that doesn't mean it's necessarily a good thing."

"But I like it here."

"But...I, uh...I thought maybe we could find a place that was new for both of us."

"But..." I began.

"Please?" she pleaded. Allie put her hand on my arm. "At least go look at it?"

I lit another cigarette. "Fine," I said. "I'll at least go look at it."

"Thank you," she said.

"On one condition," I added.

"What's that?"

I held out my cup. "Pour me some more coffee and make another pot."

"Wow," Allie said as she stood up. "You sure drive a hard bargain." She kissed me on the cheek. "You are such a ruthless negotiator."

"I learned from watching "Barney Miller" interrogation techniques."

"And it shows."

"We'll go first thing in the morning," I said. "My head still hurts pretty bad."

Allie came back from the kitchen a few minutes later. "Okay, we'll go tomorrow, but only if you feel up to it. Now I'm going for a run."

"And as soon as the coffee is done, I'll transfer it to the insulated carafe and watch you from the porch."

While Allie was changing into her running shorts and sneakers, I got dressed. She headed outside, and I buckled on the two gunbelts, then grabbed my rifle. By the time I got outside, Allie was jogging along the back wall. When she came back into sight, Gracie was beside her, and Rikki was running along the top of the wall with them. Allie smiled and waved as they turned the corner and ran along the front. She had opted to wear a shoulder holster this time. But because she had no belt loops, she used a robe tie around her waist to keep the holster and magazine pouches from bouncing with each step. Allie normally ran five laps before taking a breather.

# The Roanoke Effect

Before I knew it, she was finished. Allie took an occasional sip from the water bottle as she walked back and forth the length of the porch, cooling off.

"So what's for lunch today?" she asked as she sat down.

"Well, let me see. Your choices are gourmet canned beef stew, gourmet canned ravioli, or leftover goulash."

"As delicious as all that sounds, we should probably finish off the goulash before it goes bad."

"Then ghoul-osh it is," I said in my best Peter Lorre voice.

After lunch Allie went in to shower and change clothes. I stayed out on the porch smoking and drinking some warm herbal tea. I was still not used to drinking coffee all day, every day. After five or six cups, my stomach usually had enough, even when it was doctored with creamer and sugar. I had a pretty broad selection of herbal teas to choose from. I learned fairly early not to drink any of those that had hops or chamomile in them, unless I was ready for some sleep.

"We love you, Blake." The memory of Mom's voice hit me hard. I know they love me, wherever they may be. But why do those memories keep coming back so strong? I can't figure it out. But I had other things to think about. If Allie never got that camera figured out, and therefore never got any kind of video made, then how did her face get on my TV screen? And if her first time at Victoria was the day she brought me here after the cougar attack, then who or what had been messing with the gate the day that no one and nothing was in sight?

That night I watched a rom-com with Allie in exchange for her watching a horror movie with me. It wasn't your average, ordinary, everyday, run-of-the-mill slasher. If you've seen one of those, you've pretty much seen them all. This one was eerie, not gory. Which I liked better.

We still hadn't gone to get another foldout yet, so I was still sleeping in the recliner. And just before I drifted off for the night, Allie reminded me that I had agreed to go look at another house the next day.

"Yes, dear," I mumbled.

# Chapter 31

It was midmorning when we left to go see this other house. Allie was right: this place was similar to Victoria, only bigger. Much bigger. The outer wall was longer on all sides, as well as higher, and wider to boot. The house was two and a half stories, like Victoria, only with more rooms, and a lot more living space.

"We could bring the chickens here," Allie was saying, "plant a garden – a good-sized one – and even go get the occasional cow or pig that got left behind.

"I've never done anything like that," I said. "I've never butchered an animal, I've never gone hunting. Heck, I've never even been fishing."

"That's okay," Allie said. "I've done all that."

"But why couldn't we do the chicken and garden thing at Victoria?" I asked. "There's a lot of room there."

"True, there is a lot of room there. But what I was thinking about was more the fact that it would be new for both of us.

I walked around this mini fortress some more, but in silence. It was really nice, no question. Allie had done some research on the place when she saw a symmetrical square of Douglas fir, and parts of a wall exposed in places. And a big arched wooden gate in the middle of the front line of trees. The property had belonged to a movie exec who wanted to show that he was keeping his ostentations lifestyle private. Yeah, a two-foot thick, three-hundred-foot-square wall was a good way to keep people from being curious about anything. The wall looked to be poured concrete with a quarry rock facing, inside and out. There was even a handrail all along the outer edge of the wall, and two staircases on each wall so people could take walks, apparently. The wall alone probably cost a few million dollars.

Then there was the house. Six bedrooms, four full baths, two three-quarter baths, and two half-baths. Kitchen. Formal dining room. Living and keeping rooms. Game room, two-story library, and a self-contained pub. Oh, and a full basement. I was surprised to find that as big and fancy as the place was, it only had a four-car garage.

Because the three-hundred-foot measurement was inside dimensions, that meant there were a couple of acres inside that wall. Plenty of room for everything that Allie had talked about. The tool shed was more like a small barn. I would really need to think about this. Not at all an easy decision to make.

Back at Victoria I sat on the porch with my pipe and Scotch. I watched Rikki running around with a few other squirrels. I couldn't bear the thought of leaving that little tufted-eared squirrel behind. She had become part of my life these last several months. I'm guessing Rikki's a "she" because I saw some smaller Rikki lookalikes climbing down out of the tree one day. Then after they got bigger, they began following us on our walks. Rikki had finally gotten brave enough to come close and take a peanut directly from my hand. How could I possibly leave her behind? I asked Allie that very question. And what was her answer?

"Bring Rikki and her kids with us. There are plenty of trees for them to choose from."

We sat in silence (we do that a lot), watching the squirrels play, listening to the tree branches rustling in the breeze, and watching the cats chase the occasional leaf. I had traded the pipe and Scotch for cigarettes and my CW mix. Allie had a glass of wine. She drained her glass and poured another. When she looked at me I saw fear in her eyes.

"What's wrong?" I asked.

"I'm scared."

"Of what?"

"Cougars."

"Yeah, well, I'm not overly fond of them myself. Well, at least one in particular."

"That's why I'm scared. One almost killed you."

"And we're behind this wall here."

"But it's only ten feet high."

"It's 'only' ten feet?"

"Yes. A full-grown cougar can jump upwards of fifteen feet. Maybe more."

I choked on my drink. "They can do what?!"

"They have a vertical leap of about fifteen feet."

"Wow. I suddenly don't feel so safe anymore. Thanks."

"Please don't be mad. I didn't say that to scare you."

"You succeeded anyway." I stood up and grabbed my things. "Is this your new idea, your new plan to get me to leave here?"

Tears welled up in her eyes. "No," she whispered. "It's not."

"Then why did you not mention this before?"

"Because I was hoping you would leave because you wanted to be with me, not because you feared being attacked again."

# The Roanoke Effect

"I did want to be with you," I said. "I mean I do want..." Allie's scream cut me off in mid-sentence. I whirled around to see what was behind me that scared her so much. As if on cue, a cougar had jumped up on the wall. It crouched there, staring at us with malevolent eyes. I drew my .44s and cocked them.

"Get in the house," I said. "Now!" I whispered sharply.

The cat's eyes shifted from me to Allie to the Rotts. I heard the three of them go inside. I began working my way backwards toward the front door. The cougar let out a scream that made me go cold inside. I holstered my right-hand gun so I could open the door. I felt for the knob rather than look for it. There was no way I was taking my eyes off that big cat. My hand found the doorknob, and the door opened as if by magic. I quickly stepped inside just as the cougar leapt off the wall and ran toward the porch. For a moment I thought the entire doorframe would come out of the wall when the big cat slammed against it. Its screams and yowls filled the air as it clawed at the solid oak door. There was a security bar for the front door leaning against the wall. I hadn't used it before because I really didn't think I would need it. I decided right then and there that we absolutely did need to use it. One end of the bar had a two-inch peg that fit into a slot in the floor. The other end was a u-shape that slid up under the doorknob while the stem ratchet-locked into place. It gave me little comfort at the moment. I stood staring at the door, hyperventilating. I was obviously not over that first attack months ago. I thought I was. It had hardly crossed my mind but for fleeting seconds now and then. But this new visitor reminded me that I was indeed very much afraid of cougars. The cacophony of the cat's screams and its claws tearing at the wood was almost more than I could take. And then all of a sudden it stopped. Dead silence. My eyes went wide.

"Chauncey and O'Malley!" I shouted. "They're still out there!"

Allie's eyes widened with fright. "Oh, no! How are we going to get them back in?"

"'We' aren't. I am."

"But..."

"No 'buts'," I said. "Take the dogs and lock yourself in the library. I'll be back soon."

On the top floor were some windows that overlooked the trees at the side of the house. There was a black walnut tree that was taller than the house. Some of its branches reached the roof. I looked around to see if I could spot the two smaller cats. I didn't see them, but I also didn't really expect to. It was more like wishful thinking. But at the same time, I also did not see the big cat. But that didn't mean it wasn't still around.

"Chauncey!" I whisper-yelled. "O'Malley!"

Nothing. I tried again. Still nothing. I finally gave up all pretense and just hollered for them. A couple of seconds later I saw them dart out from under a thick shrub and streak toward the black walnut. It seemed that they didn't even touch the tree, just veered up and flew into the branches. Then my heart sank. The cougar rounded the corner of the house. It stood at the base of the tree and looked up. I watched with horrified fascination as the cat crouched and without any apparent effort jump a good ten feet and latch onto the trunk. Its claws digging deep, the cougar went after my cats. I kept calling their names, trying to get them to come toward the sound of my voice. I couldn't tell if it was working, but I kept at it. Soon my efforts were rewarded. I saw a branch start to shake a little. Then I saw both cats making their way toward me, O'Malley in the lead. The branch all of a sudden dipped as if under a great weight, Chauncey and O'Malley almost falling off. They froze, eyes wide with terror.

"Come on, guys," I urged them. My eyes went wide. The cougar was on the same branch as my cats. "Come on! Hurry up!" I was getting frantic. They began moving forward again as the cougar inched its way toward them. I kept urging my cats on, calling them, begging them to hurry up. I leaned out the window as far as I possibly could, willing them to jump to me. Almost as if they read my mind, O'Malley made the leap right into my arms. I quickly dropped him to the floor. I turned back to the window just in time to see Chauncey launch himself into the air. Just as I caught him the cougar also leapt. But the branch gave way under the cat's weight and extra force made by the jump. The cougar plummeted almost forty feet, bouncing off some limbs, breaking others. It hit the ground with a thud that I could almost feel. It didn't move.

I closed and latched the window and heaved a huge sigh of relief. I sank to the floor under the window to wait for my shaking to stop. Once I was on the floor Chauncey and O'Malley climbed my shirt and nuzzled under my chin. I decided that simply meant "Thank you."

As my heart rate slowed and the fear shakes subsided, I heard Allie's voice coming up the stairs.

"Blake? Blake!"

"We're okay!" I hollered back. "We'll be down in a minute!"

I waited a bit before deciding that I had calmed down enough. I didn't want Allie to see me like that. Male pride, I suppose. She had saved my life once already, and nursed another injury, both from animal attacks. I couldn't let her see me as a quivering mass of shot nerves. I had to at least pretend that I was still in control of myself. But I was wrong; I wasn't calm enough yet. I got up, still scared to death over what had just taken place. So much so, in fact, that after just a few steps I fell to my knees. My legs just didn't want to work.

"Blake? Are you okay? Did you fall?"

"I'm fine!" I hollered. "My leg just gave out!"

"What's wrong with your leg? Are you injured?"

"I'll be down in a minute!"

"You said that five minutes ago!"

"Okay, then I'll be down in several more minutes! The boys are fine! We'll be down soon." That last part trailed off because I was a complete and exhausted wreck.

"And the cougar?"

"I'll be down soon! I don't want to keep yelling back and forth!"

"Okay! I'll wait!"

After a couple of minutes of in-with-the-good-out-with-the-bad breathing, I forced myself to be okay. Each exhale I added an alternating "relax" and "calm down." I could feel the tension releasing as I talked to myself. I climbed to my feet and slowly made my way down to the library. Allie was standing there with the door open. As I reached the ground floor she ran over and flung her arms around my neck.

"I thought I had lost you," she sobbed.

"No, not today," I said. "And I'll do my best to not make it tomorrow either."

Allie released her death grip on my neck and kissed me. "That would be really nice," she whispered.

"I need a drink," I said. "And a smoke."

"Lose the gunbelts and sit down," Allie said. "I'll get them."

I set both gunbelts on the floor beside my chair. "My" chair. I hadn't really thought of it that way before. Not consciously, anyway. But I guess it is my chair. Actually this house and everything in it was mine. Possession, as they say, is nine-tenths of the law. Well, except for what Allie had brought. I untied my work boots and slipped them off. That's when I decided to trade them for a pair of pull-on boots instead. The monotonous repetition of tying and untying and threading and unthreading the laces had finally gotten old. Lace-ups with a side zipper would be better than these, but regular pull-ons would beat them both.

I had just kicked back in the chair when Allie came back with a tray full of stuff. A rocks glass, a wine glass, and a bottle of wine. A plate of sliced cheese and summer sausage and squares of sourdough bread. I filled my pipe as Allie poured me a double Dewar's, rocks. A match later and I had a nice cloud of blue smoke hanging in the air. Allie poured herself a glass of wine. Then she lit a cigarette.

"When did you start smoking?" I asked. "I have never seen you do that."

Allie looked at the cigarette in her hand, watching the smoke float toward the ceiling.

"This is my first ever," she said. "I thought I was going to lose you. I barely kept it together down here." She took another drag. Tears welled in her eyes as she exhaled. "I can't stand the thought of losing you."

George had taken his spot on the floor beside me and Gracie was on the couch beside Allie. Chauncey and O'Malley had resumed their usual places on the arms of the couch. All as if nothing had happened. As if a cougar hadn't jumped our no-longer protective wall. As if that same cougar hadn't just tried to claw its way through the front door trying to get us. As if that very same cougar hadn't just climbed a tree and tried to kill my cats, and maybe even me. As if, as if, as if. I looked around taking it all in. Then looked back at Allie. She was staring at the floor, and her hand was trembling. The smoke from her cigarette was not rising in a straight line, but a jagged side-to-side. I went over to the couch and sat beside her. I put my arm around her shoulders and pulled her close. She leaned over and rested against me. Then she started crying.

"Hey," I said. "I'm okay. You're not going to lose me."

Allie pulled away and looked at me, tears running down her face. "You don't know that," she said. "What if another cougar jumps the wall? What if you're not able to get away?"

I pulled her close again. "Well, it's my understanding that they can't make a twenty-foot vertical leap."

It took a few seconds, but Allie pulled away and looked at me again. "You mean...?" she began.

"Yes," I said, "We can start packing everything tomorrow."

Allie threw her arms around me and kissed me again. "Thank you, honey." Her eyes went wide.

Honey. The first term of endearment spoken by either of us.

"I...I...," she stammered.

I just pulled her close again and kissed her soundly. At least that's what I was aiming for. And I must have done something right. Allie didn't complain.

## Chapter 32

We ate the contents of the snack tray Allie had brought, then moved to the kitchen. All the while we were discussing what should be moved first. It was a pretty easy decision: weapons, food, and medicine halved, one part taken to the new place and the other left for last. Some clothing as well. And everything else was secondary. We decided that the furniture truck and the biggest U-Haul would be used for the move. Fewer trips that way.

After we ate supper, we settled into the couch to watch an old Hitchcock movie or two. I was angled into the corner of the couch with Allie reclining against me, my arm around the front of her shoulders, under her chin. We fell asleep like that before the second movie was over. The day's "activities" had taken their toll, more emotionally than anything; neither one of us moved all night. The next morning we both had a crick in our neck.

Once we stretched and got our bearings, we did our usual morning routines. After breakfast we started bagging, boxing, and crating the basement armory. On our first break we went to the U-Haul lot to get their biggest truck. A twenty-seven-footer sat at the back of the lot. I got the truck number, found the corresponding key in the office, and we drove back to Victoria. We spent the day loading the bags, boxes, and crates from the basement into the furniture truck, along with several gasoline drums.

"No more," I pleaded. "Please. No more." I sat on the bumper of the moving van. "I am done. I'm done in. And I'm done for."

Allie swiped her bandana across her forehead. "I agree. Let's go get cleaned up, and I'll fix you a nice supper."

"But what about you resting?" I asked.

"I'll rest when supper's ready. But if it makes you feel better, I'll sleep in in the morning and you can make breakfast."

"That'll work," I said.

"So what do you want for supper?"

"What are my options?"

"Meatloaf or meatballs. Same stuff, different shape. The meatloaf would be topped with a sweetened tomato compote, while the meatballs would be swimming in a delectable thickened beef sauce with sautéed shallots and white button stems and pieces."

"Tomato compote?"

"Ketchup."

"Oh. Right. Meatballs, please. With that thickened beef sauce stuff.

"Onion and mushroom gravy."

"Uh, yeah."

"Mashed potatoes?"

"Definitely."

We headed for our respective bathrooms to shower. Afterward I made a cup of herbal tea and sipped it while enjoying a long thin cigar. It wasn't bad. I had just gotten a fire going when Allie came downstairs looking as fresh as a daisy. A beautiful, strawberry-blond-haired, aqua-green-eyed daisy. She glanced my direction as she passed by on her way to the kitchen. When she saw that I was watching her, she gave me the most dazzling smile I had ever seen. I had to admit it: I was in love. I never thought it would happen again. I never once thought my heart would belong to another. And she didn't know it yet. I guess she probably had an idea, what with all the kisses and such, but no words were ever spoken. Mainly because even I didn't know how I felt. But that was then. And now I did. I put my teacup on the lamp table, my cigar in the ashtray, and went to the kitchen. Allie was just about to tear the plastic wrap off a package of ground beef.

"Hang on a sec," I said.

"Why?" she asked. "Is something wrong?"

"No. Not at all."

"Then why-?"

I cut her off when I took her in my arms and kissed her like never before. After the initial surprise, Allie slid her arms around my neck and returned the kiss. When I finally let her go, she was wide-eyed.

"Wow," she said. "Where did that come from?"

I lightly stroked her face. "It came from a place called 'I Love You'."

Her eyes went even wider than before. She bear-hugged me. "I am so glad," she said into my chest. Then looked up. "Are you sure? I mean, is this what you want?"

"Yes, I'm sure."

"Good. Because I love you, too."

I smiled at her. And I know it must have been a stupid teenage crush kind of grin. That's how it felt, anyway. And I didn't care.

"Go sit down, my love," she said. "I'll let you know when supper's ready." Allie blushed and looked at the floor. "I've been waiting to say that for a long time."

"Say what for a long time?"

"My love." She looked up. "I've loved you for a long time. That's another reason why it hurt so bad when...you know...after the cougar attack."

"I'm sorry."

"I know. I didn't say that to make you feel bad, just to explain a little more why it hurt so much."

"I would never hurt you on purpose."

"I know you wouldn't. You're a kind man. I could tell that years ago. Now go sit down so I can finish supper."

"But you haven't even started."

"And whose fault is that?"

"Um...uh...well...mine, I guess."

"Yeah. But you know what?"

"What?"

"I kind of liked the interruption."

"I'm glad."

"Now go sit down so I can finish supper."

"Well, as I mentioned, you haven't started."

"Then let me start so I can finish."

"Yes, ma'am."

I went back to the library. The fire was burning low, and the room cooling off, so I turned up the heat a few logs. My tea was cold, so I gulped it down and poured a Scotch. I relit my cigar and thought about what had just happened. My main question to myself was, Why didn't I say something earlier? That's just the things work out, I suppose. Soon Allie was back in the library.

"The meatballs are in the oven, and I won't need to make the potatoes and gravy for about forty minutes yet. Do you mind if I join you?"

"Not at all."

I hadn't put my feet up yet, so when Allie sat in my lap, I pushed the chair back to recline. She curled into a ball and rested her head on my chest. We just sat, not talking, simply enjoying each other's presence. Much too soon the timer went off in the kitchen. Allied sighed.

"I don't want to get up," she said.

"Then stay."

"If I do that, supper will burn."

"And…?"

"And then I'll have to start over, and we'd be eating just that much later."

"You do have a point."

I put the footrest down, but Allie showed no inclination to get up. Until she did.

"Supper isn't going to finish itself. Darn it."

"Maybe we could teach the cats to cook," I said.

"I wouldn't bet on it," Allie replied. She got up and headed for the kitchen. "It'll be about fifteen more minutes. So you've got that long to pick something to watch, if you want.

"Actually, I'd like to sit at the table with you. Save the TV for later."

"I would like that."

I had long since emptied my glass, so I just knocked the coal off the cigar. I'd finish it later. I can't say how many meatballs I ate that night, or how many servings of mash-pots and gravy I had. I got too busy enjoying the meal and talking with Allie to pay any attention to anything else. After supper we migrated back to the library. We wound up sharing the chair again. And I kind of liked our new seating arrangement. A zomedy followed by a William Castle thriller before we called it a night. Allie took the time to fold out the couch this time. There was no point in bringing another foldout here since we were leaving soon. We would worry about all that later. I was surprised that we made it through both movies this time, as worn out as we were.

## Chapter 33

When I woke up it was late morning. Allie was still asleep. Or so she wanted me to think. When I looked over at her, I saw her eyes close real quick. Playing 'possum, as they say. And then I saw a ghost of a smile on her lips. I made myself get up. I had agreed to make breakfast, and I intended to do just that. I shuffled my way to the bathroom to do my thing. On my way to the kitchen I stopped and leaned over the back of the couch.

I kissed Allie lightly on the cheek. "Good morning, love," I whispered. She smiled, but kept her eyes closed. Off to the kitchen I went. It wasn't too long before I took her a breakfast tray with sausage, toast, and scrambled eggs with onion, cheese, sour cream, and bell pepper. And a cup of rooibos tea.

"Wake up, sunshine," I said. "Breakfast is served."

Allie stretched and yawned. Her movements reminded me of a cat waking up. She started to get up, but I stopped her.

"Stay where you are. I have a lap tray for you."

She sat up and put her pillow between her and the couch. "Thank you," she said. "It looks wonderful."

"You're very welcome," I said as I set the tray across her lap.

"Where's yours?"

"In the kitchen. Be right back."

"Salt? Pepper?" I asked when I returned.

"Both, please." Allie inhaled deeply. "It sure smells good."

"Hope it tastes good, too."

"I'm sure it will."

It wasn't too bad, if I may say so myself. I rinsed off the breakfast dishes and put them in the dishwasher while Allie went upstairs to get dressed. Before we got started on loading any more stuff, we had a trip to make for some pull-on boots for me. The Rotts went with us, as usual, and I found a pair I liked fairly quick.

Back at Victoria the work resumed. We left two of the remaining full drums along with the empties in the garage for now. Both bigger trucks were topped off before starting with the nonperishable foods and medical supplies. Boxes and totes filled with canned and dried food were loaded into the moving truck. There was still a fair amount of room left, so I went in and just swept CDs and DVDs off the shelves into more totes. When all that was loaded, we made another check to see if there was anything else that needed to go into the U-Haul. There didn't seem to be, so I closed and latched the rollup door, and secured the ramp.

"You know," Allie said, "there looks to be enough room for a couple of the upright freezers in the furniture truck."

"I thought we were going to get all that on the next trip," I said.

"Why not use the space?" she asked.

"You sure you want to go through all that effort right now?"

"We may as well. It'd be two less uprights to get later."

"I don't know," I said. "Maybe we should wait. We're both pretty tired."

"You still have the appliance dolly out from loading the gas barrels. We'll just load one if you want."

I hesitated because I had a bad feeling. But then I looked into those aqua-green eyes again.

"Pleeeeeease?" she pleaded.

"Okay," I said. "But just one."

We got the upright freezer that was farthest from the truck and pulled it away from the wall. I unplugged it, hung the cord over the screen on the back, and cinched a ratchet strap around it. I pushed, Allie pulled, and we got the freezer tipped enough to get the dolly under it. Another strap and the freezer and dolly were one. The upright was pretty full of various meats, so it was heavy enough to be almost unmanageable.

This time, with me pulling and Allie pushing, we managed to get the freezer scooted and rolled over to the furniture truck. After a smoke break, we wrestled the dolly and freezer onto the lift.

"I sure hope the lift holds," I said.

"What are you worried about?" Allie asked. "The sticker on the arm says it's rated for over six thousand pounds."

"You never know," I said. "You just never know."

We stood on the lift with the upright. I turned and pushed the green button and up we went. The hum of the hydraulics seemed louder than usual. The lift reached bed level and stopped, swaying slightly from side to side. It stopped after a few seconds. Allie peeked around from her side of the freezer.

"Are you okay?" she asked.

That's when I realized I had been holding my breath. I exhaled slowly, trying to act natural.

## The Roanoke Effect

"Sure," I said. "Let me make sure everything's out of the way."

My back was turned for only a couple of seconds. I'll never get the sight and sound of what happened next out of my head. Ever. I heard a metallic groan, a crash, and a scream. I whirled around. The lift had broken, dumping the dolly, freezer, and Allie to the pavement. It was only about a four-foot drop, but that's all it took. I got sick when I saw it: an arm and a leg sticking out from under the deep freeze. I knew immediately that Allie was dead. As dead as Emily.

## Chapter 34

Two years now since the Nightmare began. In the six months since I buried Allie, I've lost forty pounds and my hair has turned white. Chauncey and O'Malley barely move from their perches anymore. George and Gracie seemed to age years almost overnight. Rikki's little ones have long since grown up and left the nest.

I never left Victoria. After Allie's death, I eventually got things unloaded and put back. Except for the offending freezer. I knew I had to keep the dolly, but I dragged the still-full deep freeze far away from the house and left it. I wanted nothing more to do with the thing that killed the woman I loved.

I don't care anymore. I've gone out armed to the teeth, looking for things to shoot. Wishing another cat would attack me. I'm not brave enough to end things myself.

# The Roanoke Effect

Then again, I probably wouldn't need a cougar to take me out. My food supply is running low. I'll most likely starve to death. I'm tired. I am so very tired. I just want to sleep now. For a really long time.

# Chapter 35

"And that, Senator, is how this virtual reality program works." General McIntyre gauged Senator Lumly's reaction. So far the lawmaker seemed impressed. "Except in Mr. Dornan's case," the general continued, "it will be for the rest of his natural life. At his own request. Civilian and military applications abound. A detailed report will be sent for your committee to go over. Better lay in a good supply of food and drink. It'll be a long read."

"So how did Mr. Dornan come to hear about this?" Lumly asked.

"We put it up on the local job board that we wanted beta testers. He was one of the first to sign up. He told us the reason for his strange request, and we agreed to it. Because he is a lifetime volunteer, all of his medical needs, such that they are, will be taken care of by us." McIntyre pointed to a panel of monitors. "We can see him from multiple POVs, or points of view, like in a video game." Then he pointed to one screen in particular. "This monitor is his first-person POV."

The monitor indicated by General McIntyre made them feel as if they were the ones walking and looking around. Dornan turned his head as a dog jumped at him. Lumly jumped back and spilled his coffee on himself.

McIntyre chuckled. "Yes, it's that realistic. And while he's in there, he has no recollection of having come to us about doing this. As far as Mr. Dornan is concerned, everything segued seamlessly from his wife's passing into what he's living now."

"So what happens next?" Lumly asked. "He apparently believes that he's going to die soon."

"I'm getting to that. Mr. Dornan's parents and in-laws came to sit with him and talk. The in-laws stopped coming after a short time. Even the senior Dornan doesn't come as often as before. He says he can't handle not being able to converse with his son. They moved here to make the visits easier." McIntyre moved toward the door. "Let's go out in the hall. Sometimes his mother's words seep into his subconscious. He's actually hearing her talking to him. But he thinks they're memoires from his past."

"But what if he wants to come out of the VR?" Lumly asked.

"First of all, he doesn't even know he's in a computer program. Second, we couldn't pull him out now if we wanted to. He's been in far too long at this point. Mr. Dornan is so immersed in this virtual reality that bringing him back to actual reality would be too much of a shock to his system. It would kill him. To him, it's been two years. In reality it's only been a few months."

"Okay," Lumly said, "but what about him thinking he's going to starve to death?"

"In his mind, he'll be going to sleep. Out here, he'll go under just like he would when going in for surgery. Dreamless sleep. During that time, his memory will be wiped. When he wakes up, he will find himself in a different situation. But with no recollection of his previous one. We have several to choose from."

## Chapter 36

15 August.  Sgt. Blake Dornan.  With mortar rounds falling like rain, I'm beginning to wonder if this war will ever end...